FORECAST

BOOK ONE IN THE CASTE SERIES

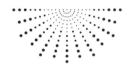

MISTY PROVENCHER

MISTY
PROVENCHER

For Those Who Seek Joy

CASTE SERIES TERMINOLOGY

Magicians: Magical children, 0-12 years of age, who have begun training to use magic.

Wizards/Wizardesses: Magical children, 12-15 years of age who have begun training to use magic.

Sorcerers/Sorceresses: Magical children, ages 16-19 years of age, who have begun training to use magic.

Witches/Warlocks: An adult belonging to the Magical Caste.

Orac: A witch or warlock, aged 20 years or more, who are able to cast their energies into the *worl*, replenish their energies, and is skilled enough to avoid most of the common dangers associated with managing the *worl*.

Unaccomplished: Magical who do not possess the extent of magic necessary to work with the *worl*.

Witch Doctor: Only one practicing doctor may exist in

a village at any one time. Two doctors practicing at once will cancel out each other's magical healing abilities.

Gypsy: A prestigious heritage of beings who live in clan groups in the Abyss and manage the Dimensions on the Dimensional Column.

Dimensional Column: The immense and colorful, vertical column located in the *Abyss* which houses all dimensions.

Dimension: An entire world created in response to a choice.

Pocket Dimension: A small piece of a dimension, laboriously crafted by Gypsies, which is attached to a regular dimension. The connection/path between a dimension and a pocket is usually connected and obscured by *vias*.

Vias: A Gypsy word meaning, *empty bridge*. Characterized by a cold and dangerously disorienting brume, the *vias* is used to connect a dimension to a pocket dimension. Gypsy Glass is used to navigate the fog, but does not guarantee safe crossing.

Abyss: The dark, outer space where the Dimensional Column exists.

Scorching: A infectious condition which prompts homicidal and/or suicidal tendencies.

Worl: The rehabilitative vortex with a protective *vias* barrier, created to contain and heal *scorched souls*.

Outer World: The regular world, which exists in the regular dimension, outside of the pocket.

Outer Worlder/Dweller: Beings who live in a dimension, outside of a pocket.

Grandmother Trees/ Grandfather Rocks: Deceased ancestors who have chosen to remain in spirit within trees and rocks, to share positivity and wisdom, through vibration, to the living. A shared characteristic of both trees and rocks is their protective tendencies.

Caste: Specific communities/groups possessing particular abilities inherent to their ancestral line or nature.

CHAPTER ONE

To the human eye, I appear alone, and nothing like a thief.

I present myself as feeble and ancient, wizened on my wagon bench, a constellation of wrinkles creasing my brow. My arthritic knuckles ache as I clasp the reins and guide my great, white Clydesdale through the drowsy, pot-holed streets of Lake Linden on this holy, summer night. Beneath me, the gypsy wagon ambles and creaks, jostling the contents within the maroon cabin, which sends up soft, muffled groans. I hum to soften the sound.

The town is quiet and warm, even though the late summer sun has abandoned the landscape. Sunday dinners were finished hours and hours ago. Surprisingly, the town's children aren't pressed against the house windows, hoping to spot the first glimpse of the coming carnival.

If they were, and if I allowed them to detect me, and if they could read, they would see my name and title, splashed across the sides of my wagon in garish, gold lettering that glitters with the glow of the streetlights. I despise the announcement. It reads: *Edeva The Fortune Teller*, which is not only incorrect, but also, most often, mispronounced. People most often say *Ed-Eva* or *Ed-Diva* and I bite my lip rather than correct them. It is difficult, since my true name, given to me by my great grandmother, sparkles off the lips like starlight when spoken correctly.

However, my name is, for now, *ED-eh-vah*. Like a belch or a curse, a name most often spit out with a lip pinned over a canine.

As for the label of *fortune teller*, nothing could be further from the truth. I'm a fortune maker, or even a fortune taker, but *teller*? It's a ridiculous accusation, considering the number of secrets I *keep*.

Not that I care about any of this. It's all the better for me if no one can recall me with any accuracy. It is treacherous. I am a woman who wishes to be forgotten.

Mulani's massive hooves clomp along and the wagon wheels grind under another street light on Calumet Avenue. The wagon is risky enough, considering my gypsy roots, but traveling with a carnival seemed like a stroke of genius. Except that the carnival master hasn't a care for my safety. He insisted upon the five foot swirl of letters, and commissioned the hideous defacing of my home. I agreed to it only because I need to keep moving, need to remain hidden just a bit longer.

Barely anyone notices the protective sigil beneath the abused moniker, the design painted as intricately as a tapestry in beautiful mustard yellows, violets, and ever-greens. I cannot reveal how I acquired the sigil, but the symbols come from a nationality every being once knew, though it has long been forgotten. It cloaks me as much as is possible, considering the name plastered on both sides of the wagon.

The rest is up to me. And I can't take another streetlight.

I reach up a hand and turn it precisely in the air, as if I'm twisting the metal pin on a sardine can. The street lights ahead of Mulani blink off. Dark, sheer veils unfurl from shadows, pouring down toward the sidewalk, covering the windows.

But one pair of human eyes, which I could never prepare myself to see, appears behind the glass of a partic-ular shop window.

The sight of them steals my breath. They belong to the young man I came to find.

I never expected him to be in plain view, or to find him so quickly.

Maybe that's why he is the only one in all of Lake

Linden who is aware of Mulani and I moving through the town streets. Even if the awareness is little more than the itchy rise of tiny hairs at the back of his neck.

However, it would do no good for him to see me like this, in the body of an old woman. My cloak of shadows must remain thick.

The young man looks up from a bucket of dish suds when the blazing street light outside Lindell's Chocolate Shoppe blinks off abruptly. All alone and closing up the store for the night, the extinguished light attracts his attention. I assume this particular streetlight, more decorative and brighter than any of the others, is as consistent as Christmas. A beacon of sorts in this cozy town, I would wager no one has ever once known it to flicker, let alone burn out.

Soap bubbles slide down the young man's arms as he walks toward the front door. His name tag says *Gavin* in thick, black letters. My breath sticks in my lungs. I knew it was him, but seeing his name emblazoned on his chest is like finding a gift with my own name written on it.

Halfway to the entrance, he stops dead. My rig's mammoth shadow, darker than even the darkness outside, sweeps along Lindell's front windows. It leaks across the tiled floor and dusts over the toes of Gavin's shoes. The blackness is so deep, he blinks at it before lifting his head to squint at what I've made sure he can't see: *me*.

Though I'm undetectable, the hotel across the avenue

could still give me away. Wildly distorted by the shadow-veil I placed over the shop window, the image of the familiar building is probably rippling in his vision like a picture painted on a gust of wind.

I tap the floor board with the toe of my shoe. The soft sound of suds dripping off Gavin's fingers flood my ears, splashing down in small, foamy puddles on the tiled floor.

"That's crazy," he whispers to himself.

Mulani's ears prick backward.

We pass the shop, but I twist on the driver bench, keeping my eyes on Gavin. I flick my wrist and the street light on the corner pops back on.

He rushes to the door, trying the handle as he peers over the closed sign. The knob is slippery in his palm and still locked. He presses his forehead to the door, but I'm certain his wide eyes only see the usual, empty avenue.

He shakes his head with an unconvincing laugh.

"I haven't even been drinking," he says before returning to the soapy dishes left in the sink.

CHAPTER TWO

Mulani assumes a trot with a sharp click of my tongue. The clapping of his hooves is undetectable to human ears, but his ears are still sloped back, unsure. I guide my great horse onto Hecla Street, flicking off the streetlights and lowering the shadow veils.

"Whoa, Mulani, whoa," I soothe and his trot returns to a steady plod. "It's time to do our work."

He flicks his ears. I reach down below my bench seat, retrieve my purple, velvet bag, and lay it beside me. Unexpected movement on the sidewalk startles me.

A squat man appears from around a corner, wiping an arm across his chin to clear his last meal from his lips. He stops dead at the sight of me and Mulani draws up short.

From beneath the splatter of the man's low-hanging sausage curls, he peers up at me on the wagon bench. His glasses are so thick in both rim and glass, it seems that it would take a great struggle to see me at all, but despite his personal impairments, and the care I've taken to travel undetected, he stares directly at what he shouldn't be able to see: *me*.

This must be the night for being seen. The fine bones in my neck stiffen with the danger of it.

Unlike Gavin, this detection is completely unexpected. I have no idea who this chubby little man is, with his dingy mop of gray curls and, upon closer inspection, a face mottled by moles. I rarely meet a soul whose intentions I can't immediately decipher, but as this man blinks up at me, I have no idea if I've found him accidentally, or he's found me on purpose.

I straighten on the wagon bench, a bead of sweat drizzling down my back. I know too well that what things seem to be are not always what they are; my quest could very well end here, at the hands of a tiny man who looks as though he couldn't defend himself against a determined gust of wind. I don't dare move until I must. The tiny neck bones ratchet to the point of snapping.

The man startles me by swiping a finger under his nose. "Now, that's a beautiful moon," he mumbles.

I turn with a grimace, half-expecting a crackling, orange shooting star to be blazing over my shoulder, but find the full, white plate of a docile moon dangling in the sky instead.

I look back at the mysterious little stranger.

He switches his gaze to the sidewalk, as if he hasn't seen me at all, and walks away at such a leisurely gait, I am mostly convinced I've remained invisible. Since he did nothing more than comment on the moon, I let him disappear around the next corner, all the while hoping I'm not making the biggest mistake of my life.

Mulani snorts, as if questioning my decision too, and I tap the reins across his back to remind us both to focus on the work ahead.

The wagon wheels creak forward. From the cavern of my wagon, a sigh whispers through the window.

"It will be soon, I promise," I whisper, just as I spot the first of the many gifts I sent to Lake Linden weeks ago.

CHAPTER THREE

The first gift I find is taped to a corner window, to the middle, muntin strip of a well-kept, charcoal bungalow. The circular branch is wrapped and crisscrossed with indigo-colored silk cord. Heather green feathers and deep blue beads cascade from the bottom of the ring.

I sent the charmed dream catchers weeks ago and this is proof that they arrived as I hoped—in mysterious places all across Lake Linden. They were found in the bottom of toy boxes, and in the trenches of school bags. They'd been discovered along the roadside like lost treasures, plucked from sock drawers, and spotted beneath furniture. Everyone questioned where they'd come from, but not for more than half a moment. The recipients of my gifts were pleased to find them and compelled to take home their prizes, displaying them in their windows.

Unfortunately, not all of my gifts are as fruitful as I would hope. The dream catcher hanging in the window of the gray bungalow is one of those. Its silk cord is empty, the feathers shedding. No dreams of interest there. I urge Mulani forward with a click of my tongue, in search of the next home with another gift in the window.

I pass home after home, only halting when I spy a dream catcher bowing the kitchen curtain rod of a white brick ranch. What look like bloated, iridescent rain drops crowd the dream catcher's silk cord and cling to the hanging feathers.

"Ah, yes." I can't help but whisper my delight and Mulani snorts in agreement.

I reach out with my open, wrinkled hand and fold my fingers inward, one at a time, starting with the pinky. The sparkling drops—each a dream, a singular desire—jiggle on the dream catcher's cords before melting through the glass. They wobble through as if the window pane isn't even there. The glinting bubbles bumble through the darkness toward me. They land in my palm, pleasingly heavy and slightly viscous.

Handful after handful, I slide the dreams into my velvet bag, twenty-six in all.

The bubbles are a mixture of dreams from the married couple living beneath that roof. Swirling my fingers over the bag, their dreams are warm and fresh, ranging from desiring a new name, to having a healthy child, to escaping the current mismanagement of their life.

I wonder if they realize how many of their dreams conflict. I pluck one bubble from the bag—hers. It seems that she desires every moment of his attention, while he wants to spend every second away from her, creating a successful business managing entertainers.

The good news is that I can help them both, even if I only help one.

I hold the dream droplet in my palm so I can consider the depth of the desire more closely. I welcome her desire to seep into my skin and as I do, my insides shift, leaving my torso feeling hollow. I've become a flesh-and-bone jar, emotions translating into physical sensation and movement. Quivers flit through me, like a minnow slapping its tiny tail in my belly.

I understand the sensations immediately.

This woman is to be a mother. Her condition is of interest to me, but it's not all that I need to know. I slip the bubble back into my bag and retrieve a different capsule of her dreams. The moment I have it in my palm, my fists clench, my eyelids flutter. She dreams of her mate abandoning his ambitions, and spending every ounce of his attention on building a family with her instead. She knows his dreams might keep him from her with long hours and prettier women. The heaviness weighing down my shoulders tells me this unrealized dream has been around a long time.

I pour her dreams into my pocket and dig around in my bag to fish out one of his. The strength of his desires immediately shoots through my skin. I can tell instantly—he is far more valuable to me than her.

The first of his bubbles shrivels in my palm as his desires dissolve into my skin. I steel myself, welcoming his dreams to permeate me, allowing my body to reveal who this man truly is, what he wants, and most importantly, what he can do for me.

My muscles begin to ache: he is a hard worker. My stomach extends, yet growls, which tells me his failure has bloated his dreams of personal gain, his need to be successful. Hunger could make him all the more dedicated to my cause, and the predominant feeling I have of his is *ravenous*. Plucking another bead from the bag, self-doubt tingles through my veins, gathering until the burn of it consumes me. I drop the sizzling desire for confidence into my pouch and draw up another dream. This one, I plant my feet. My bones are strong, solid, and pulsing with his intention for greatness. His resolution is rooted deeper than the roots of a fig tree, just as I hoped. Where he lacks confidence, he excels with determination.

The next dream has to do with his marriage. My arms wrap around my body so tightly, I cannot breathe. It is a mixture of need, want, and unconditional love that I am unsure anyone could ever fill.

I fling my arms wide. So wide, the muscles across my chest tear with the violent stretch. The desire to leave his wife, and every aspect of his current life, sail out of me as desperately as blunt daggers ripping through the skin.

This man is both scoundrel and saint, with no idea how to resolve the two. I don't know if I can help him with that.

An itch swiftly manifests in my palm. I missed it among the other impressions, but it intensifies, stronger even than the burning of his doubt.

Such a surprise this is. My interpretation of dreams is never wrong, but I am still shocked by this one.

This is the sensation of a thief. A thief, like me.

Interesting.

This man could be the greatest, or the worst, of my discoveries. His larceny is widespread; he has committed embezzlement and fraud, and believes his crimes have had no victims.

"I will take him, this Leonard Drake, I think," I whisper. "He could be awful, or he may be the most competent leader we've found. The most despicable are often also the most driven."

Mulani whinnies in clear agreement.

I have no doubt this man would not flinch at shouldering any load I give him, but how well he will handle it, I can't determine. Some things aren't known until they are tested and I sorely wish I could know for certain, but I only have time to make my best guesses.

"But I think I will leave her behind," I add.

Mulani nods emphatically, his mane leaping as he stamps the ground with one hoof.

I open my palm and the bubbles swell up to their previous size as his dreams leach out of me. When the bubbles are fat again, I blow them, like a kiss, back to the dream catcher in the window. Hers, I pour out over the road.

She will forget him the moment he enters my fortune telling tent tomorrow, when the carnival opens. She will recall that he died years ago and that her unborn is the result of a one night stand. It's a kindness, really. She will never feel the sharp blade of her husband's double-mindedness, or the wicked things he did when no one was watching.

This man will come to my fortune teller's tent on the first day of the carnival. I will make him a success, and he will never have to see her, or this town, ever again.

CHAPTER FOUR

Mulani plods to a crossroad and I honor the tug toward a dirt side street, my gifts calling. We halt at the mouth of the first driveway we encounter. A long, gravel path leads to a tiny house set far back on the lot. The structure is nothing more than a converted garage, the wide, swing-up door intact. A weather-worn door faces the road, a dream catcher dangling from the solitary window.

I can feel the dreams throbbing, before reading the crooked name painted on the lopsided mailbox: *Faye*. This is Gavin's house. Botuga, my mother's great grandmother, foretold of this time on her death bed, just as she prophesied the name of the man I'd marry.

I heard she told him with a smirk, "He will not be

Gypsy, Tonnerre. Your daughter's *given* shall be a *dweller*."

Dwellers live within the dimensions that the Gypsy clans manage on the Dimensional Column. The column is a strange thing—like an endless spine floating vertically in the black Abyss, stretching further than the eye can see in either direction. The dimensions are the column's vertebrae, each one a different, vibrant color representing the health and activity of the dimensional world within. The never-ending stacks of rainbows represent nonillions upon nonillions of worlds that the gypsy clans manage.

The number of dimensions continues to grow, because every single decision a dweller faces creates a dimension for each outcome that the dweller could choose. The dimensions multiply by the trillions each day and the gypsy clans act as gardeners, pruning the inactive and unnecessary dimensions that wither and could squeeze out active dimensions.

Active dimensions are usually the homes of the Original versions of each dweller. The Originals go into the dimensions formed from the choice they make. Duplicates populate the dimensions formed from the unchosen version of their decision and sometimes bloom into dimensions which the Original chooses to join in later choices. Gypsies must swap Originals and Duplicates while they sleep, so as to maintain a sense of normalcy for the dwellers. It's a complicated job that must be done in a timely and careful manner. After all, the death of an Original means the death of all the Duplicates in the other dimensions, so the Gypsies are also responsible for protecting Originals and valuable relics, by removing them from withering dimensions and depositing them in active ones.

As for dwellers, Gypsies adore them and look after them, but also consider them to be fragile beings with no use to the Gypsy community. They can't survive long term in the Abyss in their normal condition. My father decided, long before I was even in my mother's womb and when the clan populations were dwindling, that he would preserve our clan by insuring his children only wed Gypsies.

But Botuga had always liked to get after my father, and it didn't matter to her that she was shrunken down with age to little more than the size of a pod. She would still rattle his chain.

I was only in swaddling clothes at the time, so I could not be blamed for who I would marry someday, but my father was furious at Botuga's suggestion. So much so that if Great, Great Mama hadn't been on the brink of her passing already, and if he wasn't a revered leader, my father might've wrapped his meaty hands around her neck and helped her take her last breath.

"Great Mama! Don't say such things!" I was told that

my mother and grandmother admonished her, but Botuga only shook her head, lashing her cottony, white hair.

"He won't be a Gypsy!" Botuga insisted.

"Blessed be your crossing over, Great Mama," my father blessed her sagely, 'but my children shall only marry Gypsies. I will take a *bomfarjen* from the Pluto Clan before my Elara ever weds a dweller!"

Great, Great Mama shook her head and tilted her chin from the bedside to spit on his feet. "We must bridge the gap!"

"Gap? What gap, old woman?" my father scoffed. Gypsies never did equate the death bed with vulnerability. "There is no gap! Get on with your dying, before you leave us with only a bitter memory of a bad fortune!"

"She will marry a human dweller by the name of *Gavin Faye*, I tell you! A time will come, a time of *scorching* from a mistake of our own! Our Elara will be forced to leave the Gypsies in order to preserve us all." Great, Great Mama gathered a breath and narrowed her eyes on him. "And you will cast her out of time yourself, you tub of grease!"

"Never!" my father declared and my mother told me that she couldn't catch her breath. To be '*cast out of time*' means to be cast out of the Abyss and into a dimension. To a gypsy, that meant death.

Death, because Gypsies could no longer enter dimensions. The atmosphere would burn us upon entering it, and even if by some chance we survived, it still wouldn't matter, because we wouldn't be able to breathe.

It was our own fault that we lost the ability to travel through the dimensions. Long ago, when the workload had become too heavy for the clans to manage, so the gypsy clans enlisted Expanse Navigators to do the traveling between dimensions for them. It allowed the clans to keep control over their dimensions while cutting down on our workload, but over time, the gypsy clans stopped traveling altogether. Gypsy bodies evolved, becoming better suited to the Abyss, but we lost the ability to move through the dimensions altogether.

It was a grave mistake and I doubt there is even one gypsy who doesn't regret it to this day.

My father's brow plunged down over his eyes. "I would never send my daughter to her death!"

"Did I say death?" Botuga snapped at him. "What is now, won't be by then! I see it clearly! She is destined to travel into a dimension! We will acquire a grain, precious and rare, but with the grain, a gypsy will be able to survive in a dimension for a period of time!"

As I was told, my father turned to my mother then and whispered, "Your Great Mama is clinging, but she has one foot on the other side. Her mind is not with us any longer."

Botuga rose up on her elbows to shout at him. "You castrated gargoyle! Listen to the messages I'm delivering for you! Elara will marry a dweller and she will not be the only one! You will sanction it yourself, as it is what we *must do*, for that which we are *about to do*!"

She said this and then laid back and sneezed, her spirit rushing out of her and into the air. No one blessed her, which would have forced her spirit back into her body, because it was Botuga's time to go, and she would've killed anyone who denied her.

Un-coincidentally, the day of great, Great Mama's death was the same day her prophesy began to unfold. Warren Baro, an Expanse Navigator, crossed into the Abyss that same day and was apprehended by my people for stealing from the dimensions my people protect. Baro claimed he was searching for a particular man at the request of his cousin, who was the president in Baro's dimension. Baro had been traveling up and down the stack of dimensions in our column, but his ship also contained too many stolen objects not to be a thief.

Baro's cousin ultimately gave him over to the Gypsies in apology for the thievery and my people claimed him because we needed men to grow our population. Despite being an involuntary gypsy, Baro was given the name Lutte, of the Jupiter clan.

He is the reason I am here. *What we did* was convert Lutte Jupiter to an unwilling gypsy, and when he tried to escape our clan, he was *scorched* as he tried to return to his dimension. He is the *Original Scorched Soul*. Out of revenge, he has been spreading his infection and withering dimensions, destroying Originals, and trying to form the future to suit himself.

Great, Great Mama's prophesy came true.

My father was forced to send me from the Abyss, casting me out of time, with a precious supply of *gorne* grain that would safeguard me from incineration and allow me to breathe within a dimension. Botuga might've shocked the Gypsies with the prediction that any of us would ever be able to travel through the dimensions again, but she neglected to mention that the *gorne* would run out. It's difficult to acquire and traveling into the dimensions is a complicated, dangerous task.

I don't have a moment to waste.

I repeat the name on the mailbox three times in a throaty murmur, stretching out my hand and summoning Gavin Faye's dreams to me. It is time that I know this man who is destined to be mine.

CHAPTER FIVE

H is dreams are heavy as marbles in my palm. The first desires flood my veins, my tongue drying behind my teeth, my fingertips numb as if they are covered in tar, my ears plug up, and my eyelids are too heavy to stay open. Every symptom points to the same thing and even without the signs, I know this feeling very well. Hollow, hungering, loneliness.

I want to lay my head on my shoulder, my brain thick and heavy in my skull. Boredom. At least my chest expands, my heart pressing warmly against my rib cage. It tells me Gavin has a big heart already, but the emptiness in the rest of the body says there is room for so much more. My muscles loosen to the point that even the thinnest thread of excitement could pull me in any direction. This could be very helpful to me. I can provide Gavin the excitements of a new home, a new identity, a new life. And...ah yes, there it is...my body aching where my clothing touches it, the signal for a soul aching for change.

Gavin Faye is everything I need him to be: willing.

And I believe he is able to care for not only one woman, but an entire village.

The wagon bench bucks from a blow to the wagon wall beneath it. Mulani squeals and I duck down to croon toward the wagon wall, "Settle, my lovelies, please settle!"

A soft groan, both pleading and frustrated, weaves through the wood planks. It finds my conscience and seats itself like a guilt-paperweight.

"I am sorry, I truly am," I whisper toward the floor boards. I know they can hear me, and only me, when I whisper to them and only them. "You have every right to be restless. This journey is taking longer than I expected, but you will have every single thing I promised you and you will have it all very soon."

I've been careful to promise them everything most of them want most: roofs over their heads, food on their tables, spouses that love them, plenty of children, and a satisfying purpose. I am not fool enough to ever promise their safety, although I am always sure to imply it— anything to keep them placated.

"We are nearly finished and, if it helps, it benefits you for me to take the time to choose wisely. These men I've chosen will be yours even more than they are mine."

A collection of deep sighs from the hull of my wagon releases the tension between my eyes. They accept my promises so easily, I treasure every last one of them. I only hope they will be able to perform all the roles and satisfy the expectations I have of them.

I roll my eyes skyward, inspecting the stars. No orange stars blaze across the night canvas, no warnings from the Abyss, yet I'd be a fool to discontinue my mission. The original scorched soul continues to infect more worlds than my people can save and there must be an end to that, or there will be an end to us.

It will take a village to do what we must, and it may take even more, and possibly better, humans than I can collect to create that sanctuary. And I still have no idea if all of it will be enough to succeed.

CHAPTER SIX

Rolling through the outlying streets, the bones in my back rattle with every pothole. There has been nothing but trees for a good mile, but just as I adjust the reins in my hands to turn Mulani back toward town, I spot the distant flicker of light. Mulani plods forward, his ears alert and twitching as we come upon a rickety two-story shack with a dream catcher hanging on the cloudy glass of a front storm door.

I collect the dreams— a wasted trip, as none are what I am seeking—but as we turn back toward the road, a sharp light from a pole barn, sitting further back from the house, catches my eye. The garage door rolled up, the opening gapes.

Mulani comes to a jarring halt. I lurch on my seat, the

hitch rattles, and the contents of the wagon thunk against the wall beneath my bench.

"Yes, I see it!" I whisper to the horse.

I don't know how I didn't notice the heaviness in the air, except that I was too preoccupied with finding the last of my dream catchers. As if to verify my concern, a woman's scream shreds the silence.

"You're gonna rot for weeks before anybody bothers to come looking for you, Zelda!" a man shouts and it is followed by a horrible *thud*. The woman doesn't scream again.

I peer at the noose hanging from a rafter. It casts a long, ominous shadow across the hay-strewn floor. The rope dangles, pale and knotted, a sturdy wooden crate upended beneath it. A quiver shakes down Mulani's back, but he doesn't so much as snort.

The rancid stench of a scorched soul is in the air. Bubbling tar and burnt hair. It doesn't help to breathe through my mouth; the stink clings in my nose and throat. I choke back the gag. My instinct is to whip the reins against Mulani's back so he'll race away. I fight the impulse by tightening my fingers on the damp reins, until they cut into my skin.

This is my work. I must collect the *scorched* to insure the infection doesn't spread.

The woman may be dead already, but she won't be the only death here tonight. There is no escaping that fact, but whether it will be the scorched or me, I have no idea. There is no time for me to consult my sphere of gypsy glass and see the odds I have. This is my work—to stop the scorching from overtaking this world.

It's unfortunate that bravery doesn't dissolve terror. I force myself to set the brake. I will myself to jump down from the bench. Sharp pebbles poke through the soft soles of my shoes as I steal along the side of the house, arms flat to the shabby siding.

There is a creak from inside the barn as a humped shadow lengthens across the floor. Cloaked by darkness, I scurry across the yard and peek in the door.

A man appears with an unconscious woman slung over his shoulder. He crosses the floor and plants his right foot on the crate beneath the noose. With a heavy grunt, he heaves himself and the woman topside. Her weight pitches him forward, but he stabilizes them both.

Once steady, he reaches up and fumbles the noose over her head, tugging it down over her throat.

I step into the full light inside the doors. His head lifts at the sound of my feet scuffling over the hay, but I don't hesitate. I throw my arms over my head, wrists together.

"Tied and sound are now unbound!" I shout the spell, yanking my arms apart. The noose heeds my command. The twisted fibers spin loose like a thousand garden snakes set free from a cage. They untangle and fall to the barn floor in a heap.

I'm as surprised as the man is, but my shock is that the spell actually works, since the magic isn't my own, but borrowed. It's been unreliable, at best.

Unsupported by the noose, the man lets go of the woman too. He makes no attempt to catch her as she tumbles face-first toward the concrete. The scattering of hay offers no cushion. She lands with a sickening slap, flat and hollow.

He jumps down from the crate. The man's narrowed glare confirms his scorching; his gaze is filled with nothing but murderous rage. He doesn't spare the woman's heaped body one glance as he stalks toward me, hands tightening into fists at his sides.

"What are you doing here, old woman?" he growls.

"I'm here to help you," I say, thrusting a hand in my pocket.

His laugh is cynical. "I don't need any *help*."

He shortens the space between us in quick strides, fury twisting his features.

I have only one deadly trick left, buried deep in my pocket, saved for just such an emergency as this. But I have only one chance for it to work, and if it doesn't, this will be the unsuccessful end of my mission.

I suck in a deep breath, yank my fist from my pocket with the deadly powder clenched inside, and spread my hand in front of my face, as if I intend to blow him a kiss.

The man lunges.

I blow hard, blasting the tiny mound of hemlock dust from my palm, across my fingers, and into his face.

But the scorched man latches onto my wrist, his short nails digging into my skin. His face is coated with the hemlock, the dark powder glistening, as if it is eating holes into his cheeks, but the only other effect seems to be deepened rage. Not death.

The man's grip tightens, squeezing my wrist bones until something pops.

I scream.

He should've fallen the second the hemlock hit him. The warlock swore it would.

I am certain the terror has coated my eyes.

The scorched man laughs, but the sound is swiftly swept away in a torrent of thunder. But this storm isn't coming from the skies. The hooves of my majestic Clydesdale deliver it.

Mulani storms the barn door, crashing through the top rail, the wagon speeding behind him and shattering the lintel.

The scorched man jerks me in front of him, but I stumble and fall to the floor. Splinters rain down on us as the entire structure shakes from the wagon's impact. Mulani rears up like a white wave, his front hooves kicking at the scorched man's head.

The scorched man drops my wrist. Mulani's kick knocks the man to the floor, unconscious. I roll away as

Mulani drops down, the Clydesdale's full weight snapping the scorched man's ribs beneath my protector's hooves.

The barn goes silent.

Straw skitters as I exhale against the floor.

I push myself to my feet and drag a tiny camera from my pocket.

Just in time, too.

The scorched soul releases from the body like a cloud of opal dust. I aim the camera lens at the cloud and snap a picture. The dust falls like a plume of cold fog. That's how I know the scorched soul is now trapped on the film inside the gadget.

Mulani steps off the scorched man's lifeless body and ambles forward. The wagon rattles behind the horse, and he leans down to brush his muzzle against my face.

"I'm alright. You got him," I say. He nudges my arm over his neck and I hold on as he raises me up, pulling me gently to my feet. I lean against him and pat his neck. "Thank you, dear friend."

He whinnies and I flash him an exhausted grin. "Unfortunately, I think we must take them both now."

Mulani lowers and shakes his head. We were already tired from the travel when we came across the unconscious woman and the scorched man, but now, preparing the bodies and loading them into the wagon will set our schedule back by hours. We won't eat or sleep until dawn, but there is no choice. I must contain the body of the scorched man so any residual scorching cannot spread; I must contain the woman too, until I can determine whether she is scorched as well. I hadn't planned on taking either of them, according to the dreams I gleaned from their catcher, but now I must take both.

CHAPTER SEVEN

The parade lumbers into town the next day. The trucks pulling animal cages, along with some of the attractions—myself included—trundle down Calumet Street to announce our arrival and are greeted by wilted parents and grandparents in patio chairs, but the children squeal and shriek as the herd of clowns putter up the street on mini bikes, throwing sweets and plastic trinkets.

I am at the center of the cavalcade. The old timers point and gaze at Mulani in awe, the children clap and must be held back by parents so they don't run into the street to try and pet the great horse. Here and there, I toss my dream catchers to the adults and children who lack the familiar glow that my dream catchers impart on their recipients. My aim isn't the best and my joints are still stiff from the attack last night, but I manage to deliver catchers to those who still haven't discovered the first ones I sent along, weeks ago.

The food trucks and trailers full of gear have already made their way down Bootjack Road, over the bridge, to the open field at the corner of Valley. The sweet smell of spun sugar cones will entice the townspeople, the sound of the animals will enchant them, and roadies will call to them to play the midway games that are rarely won.

This procession is meant to pique the town's curiosity and let them know we're here. The real parade will happen tomorrow at noon, leading the townspeople back to the midway where the carnival can fleece them properly of their entertainment dollars.

The sun casts only a peach glow as we reach the end of our march and the procession circles back toward Bootjack. I knew the show would arrive late, due to trouble with one of the animal cars. I knew it, not because I foresaw it in my gypsy glass, but because I did it. The rest of the carnival performers and workers, however, collectively believe that there is some strange curse that manifests in a broken something or other that routinely delays the show's departures. They would throw me out of the carnival altogether if they knew the truth, but I do what must be done.

Following their arrival, the carnival trailers file into the open fairground field and send mice scattering with the unpacking of tarps and tents. The set up continues throughout the day and into the night, the tents rising like midnight monuments while a few sticky-faced children and their gawking parents gather to watch at the aluminum fence barriers around the field.

I situate my wagon at the farthest end of the field, at a bit of a distance from the rest of the trailers. Alfred, a roadie, collects Mulani to graze in the makeshift corral with the carnival horses and promises me that my fortune-telling tent will be resurrected within the hour.

I start a tiny fire and heat my pot of dark beans and gritty gorne. If it were only a matter of taste buds, I would skip the gorne, but it is the only reason I am able to breathe and not burst into flames in this atmosphere. I mix in some mesquite to hide the flavor.

As I stir, the silver disks lining my wrap touch together and sing like soft, celebrating bells.

"No parties just yet," I hushed them. "And as I've told you, I need you to remain silent. We don't want to attract the Blackened Soul."

The disks silence.

Once my dinner is hot enough, I retreat to my wagon. Remaining fireside is as good as inviting the ring master to approach with more of his obnoxious requests to "improve" what he calls my "act".

I climb the wooden steps of the wagon's back porch, the structure squeaking and shifting beneath my weight. I touch the arch of the wooden door with my elbow and the discs at the edge of my shawl chime. The unlatching of the lock is audible. The door swings open without my hand on the knob.

Closing the door isn't as easy. It requires a shove that throws dull, silver sparks through the darkness. The sealing charm keeps the door shut and sealed tight, against the strongest of men, as well as any tools that might be wielded against it, until I decide to open the door again.

Inside, I settle into the only space available. It is a wood chair stuffed in the corner and surrounded on every side with bulging bolts of fabric. I take my drawstring bag from beneath the chair and lay it in my lap, carefully reaching in and withdrawing a large, silvery bauble.

"Show me the man to whom my heart will be given," I say. The glass is cool against my hand as I stare into it. The vision within the sphere wobbles to life like a sparkling, silver soap bubble in my palm.

The image is of Gavin Faye. My *given*.

I watch him as I eat, although the beans are tough and the gorne tastes like old shoes. It's lovely to watch him in this way, unaware. He makes himself a sandwich and sits on the couch in his tiny house. There is a hole in his sock. As he watches the bright, square tube in front of him, his grin is handsome and his laughter is easy and light.

A warmth spreads through me that I haven't felt in decades. Observing him this way is almost scandalous, but

I can't look away. This is the quickest way for me to know who he truly is. It's also the closest we'll ever get to courting, since I'll have to enchant him promptly, the moment he agrees to be mine.

Or, even if he doesn't.

As I sit and ponder the possibility of his not choosing me, Gavin's name emerges from the sphere in a whisper. I tip my ear toward the glass, straining to hear it once again, in case I misheard the first time, and the bauble clearly repeats his name.

Gavin...

"You know what this means," I trill to the nearest roll of fabric. "He's chosen the same line of fate as ours! I will arrange for him to meet with me tomorrow!" I bolt upright with a renewed energy, and this old body aches with the swift movement. I rub my back with my gnarled hand.

The future is a fluid thing, constantly stirred within a cauldron of whims, but Gavin Faye is meant to be the cornerstone of an entire new future for all of us.

CHAPTER EIGHT

My tent is standing before dawn, long before the real parade begins. The flap is tied open and the beaded curtain wafts silently in the slight breeze. The beads will only speak if they detect a threat nearby.

The silver disks at the edge of my shawl are another story. They resonate with a soft, tender sound, something like nervous laughter. The sound of it tickles in my stomach. I would do more than smile if my arms didn't ache with the weight of the gypsy glass ball I've carried across the fairgrounds.

I brush aside the bead curtain and make my way around my fortune-telling table. It is a broad wagon wheel of plywood tacked to a barrel filled with cement blocks. The ring master insisted the table be large, circular, and hard to tip over, so I would have a head start when facing disgruntled customers.

I snort at the thought. It may be the one thing the blasted ring master got right. People seeking fortunes only fret when they are delivered the callous truth. No one pays for truth, so I rarely deliver it, but if I do, the table may prove to be invaluable.

Revealing *fortunes* is very different from revealing *truths*. A *truth* may appear in my glass ball as a dead dog, while a *fortune* encourages appreciation of unconditional love. *Truth* may be getting crap-canned from a job and thrown out on the street, while *fortune* only speaks of a new business opportunity and a change of scenery on the horizon. *Truth* may reveal a lover leaving, but *fortune* promises a new and better choice of lovers to come.

Truth is only the fact of a situation. *Fortune,* however, is a projection of faith. And *fate* is simply the outcome, once a decision is made between the two.

I haul my crystal ball onto its pedestal with a grunt. The moment it's seated, the glass fogs with a substance called the vias—a mist that separates dimensions. It clears as I concentrate on it, showing me the options and versions of my truth.

Today there is only one image that presents itself in the ball.

Gavin Faye crosses the fairgrounds, straight toward me, like a targeted missile. The image startles me at first glance, Gavin's eyes locked on mine as if he can actually see me as he weaves through the row of food trucks and empty freak show tents, ignoring the roars of caged animals that weren't taken along for the parade.

A squirm of pride wrestles my spine at the sight of him. No one is supposed to be on the grounds yet, since the parade is still plodding through town. I'll catch a mouthful from the ring master for not taking part in the procession, but I knew Gavin was coming. I'd risk everything before missing out on the chance to speak to him without children bumbling into my tent, or starry-eyed girls giggling outside. I need a moment to speak to Gavin alone, and according to the image in my crystal, the opportunity is making a beeline to my tent.

This man, with his determined stride and intense gaze, is my fortune, my fate.

I stand, smoothing down my skirt and tucking the loose, gray hairs from my temples beneath the cap of my bandana. I go to the open tent flap and push aside the silent, beaded fringe. The disks at the edges of my wrap sing a song that warms my belly.

Gavin is handsome in his worn blue jeans. Seeing him move across the fairgrounds with my own two eyes, rather than through the glass ball, is like stepping out of shadows and staring directly into the sun.

Gavin spots me right away, as he should, since I reach into my pocket, finding the smooth bubble of the desire I stole from him. I roll the droplet between my fingers like a magician about to perform a trick. The dream calls to him. I'm surprised he's not running.

I smile the moment our eyes met, but as he nears I see the dark scowl painted over his lips. He comes to an abrupt stop in front of me, the toes of his boots nearly touching mine.

"I don't know why I'm here, but I am." His tone is a solid block of anger, dipped in a brittle coat of annoyance. Even so, it's good to hear the rich decibel of it. A man with a deep voice is a man of deep convictions. I can understand his confusion over being drawn to my tent.

"Come in," I say, stepping aside. The disks at the edge of my shawl trill together. I remove my hand from my pocket and pull the beads aside in welcome.

"Just looking around, ma'am," he answers with a shake of his head.

"First reading of the day is always free."

He shakes his head again, though his gaze remains as intense, as if he senses something beyond my old crone exterior. "Nah. No offense to you, but I don't believe in it."

"Have you ever had your fortune read by a true gypsy?" I ask, reaching back into my pocket. The bubble of his dream vibrates against my skin, and I know he won't be able to resist, so it is surprising when he backs away from my tent.

"Never had it read at all," he says. "If it isn't hokum,

then I don't need someone telling me what my fate will be anyway. I can decide it on my own."

"We agree then—your fate is always up to you, so you've got nothing to lose." The silver bubble pulses in my palm. His eyes aren't the kind that stop my gaze at their threshold, but welcome it in and swallow it. "Besides, a free reading is better than the roadies banning you for trespassing before the fair has opened for business."

I tilt my head in the direction of the group of roadies headed in our direction. In all honesty, the roadies couldn't care less about trespassers, but it does the trick.

Gavin slips past me, into the tent. "You said, *free,* right?"

The silver bubble in my pocket thrums so hard it might burst.

Gavin takes the seat across from my crystal ball.

CHAPTER NINE

The *vias* within the ball is already swirling, even before I can take my seat. A very, very good sign.

"A great fortune awaits you," I say.

He scoffs. "Around here?"

"No, not here. You will choose a path that leads away in the near future, and you will travel a great distance in your old age."

"I doubt that very much, ma'am. I'm not one for traveling, but it wouldn't matter, even if I was. I've got a job and a mortgage to answer to."

"There is so much in store for you." I hesitate, almost letting his name slip from my lips, but I catch it in time. "You will answer to a far more prestigious job, young man, and possess a larger dwelling than you currently own. You will also have the woman you desire. An exotic beauty who will be your entire universe."

It's a bit abrupt, but the parade will be finished soon and the crowd will be pouring in. I regret it less as he perks on his seat. Just as quickly, he forces himself to relax, as if he doesn't want me to notice his interest.

"You may not be a wanderer, young man, but you'd travel to the ends of the earth for her ... and beyond that, if you had to. That's the kind of man you are." I grin over the top of the ball and then I remember that my teeth are not sparkling, or white, or even straight. My wrinkles may appear less charming than repulsive. What he sees, and who I am, is not aligned at this moment. I gaze back into the ball. "You will dream of her name tonight."

It is the last bit of affirmation I need to move forward. He must subconsciously choose *me,* by dreaming my name.

He kicks back in the chair with a smirk. "You're selling one heck of a fairy tale here, aren't you?" he drawls. "I bet the girls just eat up this stuff, don't they?" He laces his hands over his chest and bats his eyes. "Let me dream of my soul mates name!"

I grow stern with the insult. "I am telling you the truth, Gavin Faye."

That gets his attention. He sits up straight and leans toward me with narrowed eyes. I'm slightly grateful for the width of the table. His throat bobs with a gulp. "I never told you my name, ma'am."

I take my own gulp, hidden behind the glass ball, and struggle to hold my ground. "If you dream of a woman's name, as I've told you, then you must return to speak with me again tomorrow. If your dreams don't reveal her name, then you were right. This is all hokum and it will be the first and last time we meet."

His color dissolves as he bolts out of the chair. "How do you know my name?"

"I'll tell you tomorrow," I promise softly. "Now, go."

Gavin Faye's eyes are wild, as if I've just plucked a string in his soul. He tears out of my tent as if being chased.

Maybe revealing his name was a bit too much.

CHAPTER TEN

I wake on the chair in my wagon before the sun rises. My old bones crack and pop as I retrieve my crystal ball and the fabric napkin from beneath my chair. The napkin bulges with briny hunks of hard cheese and salty peasant bread, which I prepared the night before. Never eggs. They leave a sour taste in my mouth and cheese is much more portable. I grip both items close to my chest as I exit the wagon, worried that my arthritic fingers will fail me, letting loose of the precious cargo.

The wood creaks as I climb down the steps in the dark. My skirts soak up the dew as I make my way across the fairgrounds toward my tent. Bugs buzz in the overhead lights, strategically placed to deter thieves.

I draw back the beads covering the tent opening and stumble backward. Gavin Faye is seated on the chair inside, as if he never left. He jumps up, walking toward me. He's wearing the same clothing he wore yesterday and there are dark rings beneath his eyes. A shock of hair sticks up over his temple as if he's been trying to yank it out.

"How did you know?" he asks.

I'm still breathing hard from lugging my crystal ball across the fairgrounds, and now I clutch the cheese and bread to my chest, crushing them against me in the napkin.

"You startled me!" I breathe, but Gavin Faye isn't deterred.

"How did you know my name?"

I make my way into the tent, around him, and to my side of the table. I balance the ball on the waiting stand, releasing it from the grip on my forearm and ribs, like a giant egg. "I'm a fortune teller—"

"The truth," he says.

I sit down with a groan. It's not dramatics—the long walk really takes it out of this old body. "Yes, let's have the truth. What is her name?"

"Elara," he whispers. My soul flutters. "Tell me how you knew I would dream it!"

I motion for him to sit as I spread out the napkin with the bread and cheese between us.

"Have some," I say. "I didn't have a chance to eat this morning, so you're welcome to have breakfast with me."

"I don't want food! I want to know how you knew my name and how you knew I'd dream of *her*!" he barks.

"There's no need to speak to me like that," I tell him stiffly, breaking off a sliver of cheese and putting it in my mouth. "And what you want to know is not how I know what I do, but how you can *find* her."

Gavin drops onto the chair. He combs his fingers through his hair.

"Yes." His tone is weary. "Yes, I do."

"Now we're getting somewhere. One moment," I rise and waddle on my sore feet to the curtain wall behind me. The curtain is thick, and hung in such a way, customers assume it is the tent wall, instead of a partition where I can disappear, if the need arises. The exterior wall of the tent is actually coiled like a hose, providing a hidden exit.

Today, it will be used for the opposite: a dramatic entrance.

Once behind the curtain, I take a small sack from my pocket. I work the leather drawstring open, my crooked fingers stiff. The burnt smell of the ground constellation dust fills my nostrils with a sharp, sweet tang. Mixed with petals of dark *ambience* and the fizzle of a comet, I take some in my hand and reach up, sprinkling the dust and petals over myself.

The dusty mixture sticks to the pale wrinkles of my skin, coating it.

And then, it begins.

The color of my skin deepens first, before the planes of it smooth and settle. A sparkle emerges from the dust—a lovely golden glow that migrates into a twinkle. I hadn't realized how milky my vision was until it clears. My hair darkens and spills over my shoulders in thick ringlets. I knew the horn-ambience-fizzle mixture would transform me back to my true self, but instead of feeling like I've returned to my old self again, I feel brand new.

I take a deep breath and shed the outer layer of my clothing. Turning the discarded wad inside out and around, I give it a good shake. From the crone rags I wore, a sparkling blue dress spills out. I lift it over my head and let it flow down over my hourglass shape. It's strange, not having to tug a garment over my previous, bread-dough curves. Edeva is gone and I am finally *Elara* again.

My gypsy name, my true name, sparkles in my heart like the beacon of a lighthouse.

It is time to reveal my true self to Gavin. I only hope he doesn't bolt from the tent when he sees me, since he's seen me once before, as I walked through his dreams last night and whispered my name in his ear.

With another breath, I move from between the hidden wall and into the tent.

Gavin's gaze roves over me at first, but then he shoots up from his chair, the expression slipping off his face like a mudslide. He stumbles backward toward the beaded door.

"What's going on? Where ...where did you come from? Where's the old lady? This can't be happening!"

His body is so rigid, I think the truth might crack him in half. I improvise.

"Are you talking about my grandmother?" My voice is as smooth as a cat's tail as I draw my head back. "She told me to come out and meet you. She said there was a young man here who wished to speak to me, but I don't want to disturb you. Would you like me to go?"

"No!" Gavin sputters, wiping his palms down the thighs of his jeans. "I mean, no, please don't go."

I don't think he could take his eyes off mine if he tried. My own gaze is paralyzed.

I slide into the fortune teller's seat. The solid, orange blaze of the sun cuts through the beaded curtain and falls across the table, spilling over a loaf of fresh bread and a soft, yellow wheel of cheese. The horn-ambience-fizzle mixture must have wafted off me and over the table.

Gavin only blinks at me. I'm sure he's still taking in the woman who appeared in his dreams hours ago.

I cut the cheese in wedges. Gavin smiles as I hold out a triangle to him.

"I made this myself," I say. "Would you have some?"

He takes the triangle without protest. He puts the cheese in his mouth, and as he chews, he grimaces. The salt is kicking in. I offer him a slice of bread, which takes without hesitation, likely hoping it will relieve the dehydrating salt of the cheese. He gulps down the bread and coughs into his hand. I salted it so much, I'm surprised his cheeks aren't caving in, but he's eager when I pull the flask from my pocket and offer him a drink.

"My grandmother insists on extra salt. I don't think she has taste buds any longer," I say as he gives me a dry smile and chugs from the flask.

He takes the flask from his lips, holding it upright, as he wipes his mouth on the back of his hand. For a moment, I think the enchantment potion has kicked in full force and he's going to profess his love for me, but he only grins. And takes another drink.

I take the flask from him and take a drink myself. The first sip slips down my throat and my heart breaks. I ignore it, tipping up the bottle and taking a full, deep swallow. My interest in Gavin multiplies, questions about him filling my head, *what's his favorite color, food, music, scent?* My desire for him swells. The nerves in my stomach tense and tickle me, forcing a broad smile across my lips that I can't tame. We sit staring into one another's eyes, reaching into the depth of the irises, until the sun is fully up and the fairgrounds squirm to life.

Gavin's brow breaks as I stand.

"Don't go," he pleads.

He shakes his head, as if trying to clear his mind, likely realizing we haven't spoken a word, although it feels like volumes have passed between us. I didn't read his mind, but staring into his eyes, I could argue that I have.

"Clients will be coming to hear their fortunes soon," I say. "My grandmother needs her tent back."

He stands too, moving around the edge of the table until we're standing toe to toe.

"Come with me," he says. "I'll show you around town. I'll buy you lunch and take you to a movie."

He makes my heart ache, but there's no way I can leave the tent empty. The other dreamers should be coming to see me today. "I can't. I have to assist my grandmother."

"Then I'll stay at the carnival and we can...talk...whenever you have a break."

"I don't get breaks," I say with a sympathetic grimace. I've waited so long to be in love with him, and now, I'm unable to spend every moment with him.

Gavin throws up his hands. "Then when can I see you? This can't be the only time!"

"Tonight," I tell him. "When the fair is over."

"Midnight?" He perks at the suggestion. The romance of darkness brings his tone to life. He is thinking of kisses —I know it by the way he stares at my lips, the way he licks his own as he does it—and the prospect send comets blazing through me too.

"I'll be back for you at midnight," he says, slipping from the tent.

The metallic bead in my pocket sings itself to sleep, the dream of us suspended, until the sun gives way to a glorious night.

CHAPTER ELEVEN

Gavin doesn't honor my request to leave the fairgrounds.

All day, I catch glimpses of him poking around, his gaze always cast in the direction of my tent, squinting as if he can see beyond the beaded entry. Not that he would ever see me, even if he did, since I have donned the old bones of Edeva, the fortune teller, once again.

I watch him war with himself from across the lot, taking one step toward the tent and then spinning on his heel to take a step away. He never gets more than one step before turning back toward the tent. Hands hanging at his sides, shoulders drooped, my heart breaks with the sweetness of his desire and his inability to do anything about it. The intensity is part of the courtship, but it is also necessary since I have work to do, weeding through the dreamers, whose collected desires call them to my tent.

For such a small town, Lake Linden turns out to be my largest collection yet. I find a skilled man named Eron, with a cruel and crafty slant to his mouth; another named Braith, who barks rather than speaks; the town seamstress, named Marlyn; and a particularly cautious man who won't tell me his name at all, but only holds his mouth in a tight, grim line when I ask for it.

Each of them has great value to me, all with one skill, or several, that will prove handy; all with an interest in growing a village in one way or another; and all seeking to escape the old and begin anew.

The process of collection is a fairly friendly one. I charm their minds into a paralytic state, attach two of my shawl disks to their clothing, and instruct them to depart through the back exit of the tent and go directly to my wagon. The doorway grants them entrance with the tinkling of my disks. Once inside, my collected locate the shelf to the right of the door. They take down a bolt of brocade, and proceed into the depths of the cabin, where they roll themselves up in the cloth and fall down upon whichever lot of previously rolled bodies are stacked closest.

There, they hibernate, in the wisp of consciousness that lies between slumber and coma. There is where they shall also remain, until we reach our final destination.

The work of identifying the selected, deciding their value, and charming those I choose would be taxing enough in my younger form, but in this withered husk of Edeva, it's utterly exhausting. I don't know how I will have the energy to meet up with Gavin once the fair closes. As it is, I nod off four times while relaying fortunes to standard ticket-payers, one of whom demands her money be refunded.

I spy Gavin, walking past the tent with his fists buried deep in his pockets, as one of my last customers, a woman with a thick, winding blond braid, enters the tent. She plops onto the chair and my crystal ball smokes up inside. Not a good sign at all. She slides the obligatory strip of tickets toward the pile of tickets in the center of the table.

"I need to know what happened to my sister," she says with a sniffle. She wipes her nose with her open palm, straight up and over her forehead, across her white-blonde bangs. One of her front teeth is wedged sideways in her gum line, pushed against the other like a broken barn door...which is also the image that emerges from the gray plume inside the ball.

I draw a breath.

She leans forward, hands on the table. "What do you see?"

"An escape," I tell her. "An escape from an abusive man!"

Rather than joy, the young woman's face crumbles. "I

knew it. I knew it and I didn't do nothin' about that filthy rat!" She drags another sniffle onto her forehead, leaving a sheen between her eyes. "Where is Zelda now? Where'd she go? And where's her skunk of a husband at?"

I have no idea what the skunk's name is, but his dead body is wrapped up in the back of my wagon, and his *scorched* soul is locked up tight inside my camera, stuck to a roll of film like a fly on a glue trap.

"He will not harm her again," I say.

"'Cause he's dead? She killed him and ran, didn't she?"

I've never had anyone guess the truth so accurately. Telling her the truth would hardly set me free, but most likely get me killed, or jailed at the very least. I massage the ball with my fingertips.

"She has found herself a safe haven, but the location is too obscure for me to see. She must want to stay hidden," I say. That's a fair fortune. I haven't seen our final destination in the flesh myself—only in the depths of my glass ball, and Zelda will certainly be safe there, whether or not she is also *scorched*. "He was not himself at the time of their parting. He is seeking rehabilitation—"

The sister throws herself back in the chair with a snort. "He needs it!"

I stare at her over the top of the ball, my eyelids heavy.

"Are you getting another vision?" the young woman asks.

"No," I say, fighting a yawn. "The ball has cleared. I

have nothing else to tell you, except that your sister is safe and apart from any abuse."

"Good enough." The woman rises from the chair. "She probably checked herself into the hospital in Marquette, like before. Thanks, lady."

She walks out of the tent and into the dark night as I release a long, deep breath. The last customer of the night and it couldn't have come too soon. I place my palms on the table and am just about to heave myself up when a broad, young buck emerges from the shadows, the beads shrill as he shoves them aside and stumbles into the tent.

"My turn," he says as he falls into the chair.

CHAPTER TWELVE

T his last one of the night smells flammable. The pungent, wet stain down the front of his shirt tells me he's spent some quality time in the beer tent prior to this visit.

He throws an elbow over the back of the chair and laughs.

"I thought this was the john," he says.

"The restrooms are located—"

"Look," he drawls, "I just wanna know if I'm gonna get laid tonight." He turns his head to the open tent flap and guffaws, as if there is an audience of drunken friends outside, but there is only the empty darkness. What disks are left at the tip of my shawl trill as my crystal ball boils with deep, gray smoke.

"No, you won't be getting laid tonight," I tell him with a grimace. "That's three tickets."

The buck pulls back. "I ain't givin' you three tickets for that!"

"It's five just to step inside the tent, but I have nothing more to tell you, so I'm letting you off cheap."

"According to you, lady, I'm not getting off at all!" He glimpses behind him again, at nothing but the shadows that lay beyond the shrilling ropes of beads draped over the tent opening.

I gulp a breath, scanning the uncovered skin of his forearms for the telltale tattoo of *scorching*. It's hard to see much, since his shirt sleeves are rolled only midway up his forearms. I only hope the door beads would be clanging much harder, and my crystal ball would be flashing the fili-gree markings, if the buck were truly one of the *scorched*.

The hidden tent partition is right behind me, but if the young buck is *scorched,* I need to stop him right here and now. I run my crooked fingers down my skirt and into the pocket where I kept the hemlock dust. It's only when my fingertips hit the bottom seam that I remember I already used up my supply on the man who was trying to murder Zelda.

The buck's gaze glints, as dark as jet stone, and not one twinkle of joy in it. He shrugs. "I ain't into old ladies, but for ten bucks, all I gotta see is the back of your head."

I crouch over my sphere of gypsy glass, pouring my

anger into the ball. My eyes are the only things that rise up to meet the young buck, but the glass magnifies my emotion and projects an image over me, as real as Edeva's skin. I appear as a lion, crouched to attack.

But if he registers the vision, he doesn't show it. His drunkenness may lend him courage, or it might neutralize my extraordinary projection. Whichever it is, the buck only squares his shoulders in return, tucking his chin, like a bull ready to charge the matador.

I only have one trick left, and it's not even a trick. It's the worst I can do and I hope it is terrible enough. The interior of the crystal sphere roils.

The young buck's truth surfaces.

"Three nights from now, you'll be *getting off*," I whisper over the top of the churning, obsidian ball.

The buck takes a step to the side of the table, in my direction. His lips twist in a terrifying grin. "Now that's what I wanted to hear."

"Your father, Terence, will be the one *getting you off*." I drop my voice, letting the anger within the gypsy glass stream up through my neck and pour out of my mouth.

The buck's feet stutter to a halt. His grin drops. The color of his skin turns from ruddy to pale as I continue.

"Let me spare no details in this truth of how you will *get off,* since this isn't the first time, but it will your last. Your very own drunken father, will return from the pub in just three, short nights. He will be saturated with the smell of Jack, the same way you stink of beer right now. The moon will be high. Your mother will be sleeping. You will hear the car engine and the familiar scrape of that dented, right, front fender against the wheel—"

The buck gasps.

"But you won't be able to escape. Your own father will *get that head right off* your shoulders, boy. You are listening now, aren't you? Every woman...every animal...you've *gotten off with*, will feel the blissful release of your final breath. You can try to hide, but I must tell you, the truth is determined to *get you off*." I crest my eyebrows in consideration. "Maybe it won't be a car accident, but maybe Terence *gets you off* with the shotgun he keeps for deer season? Or a brick from that unfinished garage, when he mistakes you for a burglar, or—"

The buck sways in his boots. His dehydrated tongue darts over his lower lip, leaving no shine.

"You're fulla shit," he rasps.

I smile. "It will be a cat-and-mouse game. Your justice today is your unfortunate truth, *Colvin Jerome Minford*."

His already pale skin turns a dour gray.

"You'll see the headlights coming, and you'll run. Or, you'll see the barrel of the rifle, and you'll run. Or you'll see the brick in his fist, and, oh my, will you ever run. You are going to run, but you'll never outrun your truth, you miserable rapist. You can feel the truth beating in your chest right now, can't you? You have no fortune, Colvin

Minford, because the truth is, you are *getting off* this planet for good, in just three, short days."

The buck's lips twist. He clenches his fists as he staggers toward me. "I'm gonna beat ya to death, ya old crone!"

"You first," I say, lunging for my crystal ball. I hope these old arms have enough strength left in them to lob the glass at Colvin Minford's head.

The beaded doorway shrieks.

Gavin bolts through the fringe, grabbing hold of the buck, dragging the stunned man backward over the folding chair and out of the tent. Minford's shirt comes up over his belly as he's dragged across the ground, pebbles embedding themselves in his skin, as if I've called the stones for help myself. Gavin holds tight, heaving Colvin Minford back with one mighty rip of the shirt fabric, before sinking a damaging kick into Minford's side.

The ruckus attracts four roadies, including the man who helps care for Mulani. I've never been happier to see them.

"You got some trash that needs taking out, Edeva?" Alfred asks, casually spitting on the young buck as Colvin Minford rolls onto his stomach and vomits in the grass.

"Please," I say, and they drag the moaning buck away, leaving Gavin and I standing together in the moonlight.

CHAPTER THIRTEEN

"A re you alright, ma'am?" Gavin asks, taking my forearm.

I've forgotten I'm a frail old woman. My knees immediately respond with an ache.

"I'm fine, thanks to you. I see what my granddaughter likes about you," I say, laying my hand on his and bringing us to a halt outside the tent opening. "She was in the back, changing, when that awful boy came in. Let me go inside and tell her you're out here waiting."

Gavin mops his brow and nods with a relieved sigh.

I go into the tent, calling for Elara as I disappear between the layers of the partition. Emerging from the beaded fringe moments later, I'm still brushing the comet dust from my arms.

The new shawl I'm wearing is lined with lovely little

bells that glisten and chime as softly as the glow of the moonlight.

"It's so good to see you. I've been waiting all day and I could hardly stand it," Gavin says. He seems a little embarrassed to sound so desperate, and even though I know it's probably the enchantment potion talking, my heart twirls in the spotlight of his attention all the same.

"I've been waiting for you all my life." I laugh as if it's a joke, but it melts away any remaining tension between us all the same.

He holds out his hand.

"I don't know what to do next," he mumbles. Embarrassed again, he quickly corrects with a flick of his chin and by ruffling the proffered hand through his hair instead. His deeply masculine tone returns. "I mean, for a date. We can walk around the fairgrounds, if you don't want to leave with me."

"We can leave," I say, reaching for his hand.

His fingers engulf mine as if he's cradling a baby bird. "You're not worried about being alone with me?"

"Not at all."

"You should be afraid of *any* man who asks to take you out at midnight," he says.

I scoff. Little does he know that while I'm in my true bones, I have no fear of any regular man. The only thing I fear is a scorched soul.

We pass the dark tent of the Mollusk Man, whose skin

has hardened around his back and sides like a seashell, and cross behind the magician's tent, lights flashing within.

The enchantment potion tingles my stomach again. I crave Gavin's gaze in the same way I have craved *gorne* to breathe, and joy to live, and comfort to thrive.

It is the gypsy way to be enchanted, but the stories my mother and aunt and great mama and great, great mama told me could never prepare me for the torrent of joy that washes over me every time Gavin looks at me or speaks to me or reaches for my hand. Every century I endured, waiting for the experience of loving someone else as much as I love myself, was worth it.

"You shouldn't trust a person so easily," he says. "What if you'd gone out with the guy who was in your grand-mother's tent tonight?"

"I would never," I laugh. "You forget that I'm the granddaughter of a fortune teller. It's in my blood to know things, and I know who I should be afraid of."

"Your grandmother didn't," he says.

"Oh, I knew," I assure him with a grin. I realize too late that I credited myself, but Gavin only squeezes my hand.

"You did? What else do you know, Elara? Tell me everything."

"Everything? That's only possibilities," I say, but I sense it stealing a bit of the light from my eyes to say it. I know what is to become of us—it's the gypsy way as well

—but I don't want to spoil any of these breathless moments with the inevitable loneliness.

"Tell me why it turned me inside-out when I saw that kid in your tent mouthing off to your grandmother like that. I've only just met you, and Colvin Minford is nothing to snot at, but," his jaw tightens as he speaks, "I feel like I could beat him all over again, just thinking of it."

"You were being chivalrous," I say, tugging him toward a refreshment truck with a sign on top that reads, *Sweet Somethings*. I rap my knuckles on the truck's back door. It swings open, and a chunky, aproned woman with frizzy brown hair looks out with a frown.

"We're closed," she says.

"I'm Edeva's granddaughter," I tell her, wondering if it will make any difference.

It doesn't. "Your granny's the fortune teller? Ya know, she never done me one good reading without makin' me pay somehow. I don't see as I owe her, or you, a danged thing."

I only asked her for some sweets in exchange for the reading, but she didn't like the fortune. The problem was she didn't want to hear anything less than Lenny Kravitz breezing onto the fairgrounds and plucking her out of her dessert wagon to wed her on a beach in the Bahamas. She didn't want a fortune, and she didn't want the truth if it wasn't about her and Lenny. She's hated me ever since.

Fingers on the handle, she's about to retreat and slam

the door shut, when I lean forward and blow a sweet breath of my enchantment in her face. It's a gift, really. And the feelings that Gavin generates inside me, I feel like I have enchantment to spare.

The woman shifts, her weight rolling from one hip to the other, the door still hanging open. "Whaddya say you want, now?"

"Vanilla coffee," I say. "Two please."

"Swizzle cakes too," the woman say with a wink to Gavin. "You need some swizzle cakes, sweet cheeks."

The smile drops off my lips, but she disappears into the truck, leaving the door hanging open. A minute later, she hands me the two steaming cups of vanilla coffee and pauses with her hand on Gavin's as she passes him a plate heaped with swizzle cakes.

They're only cinnamon rolls with colored icing, but she looks heartbroken when Gavin only glimpses at her long enough to give a rushed, *thanks a lot.*

"Thanks for stopping by," the woman lingers, hanging out of the truck as she twists her hair around a finger, but I reach around and grab the door.

"Thanks again," I say as I swing it closed.

She tries to hold it open with her palm, but Gavin gives it a shove with his elbow and the door slams shut.

"That was weird," He says, but his smile ripples with excitement as he looks at me. The ripple spreads through my whole body as we walk away from the food trucks, around the edge of the fairgrounds, finally coming to a halt at a splintery picnic table just short of the makeshift corral. Mulani lifts his head and gives me a sheepish whiny. I ignore it.

A tiger in its cage relaxes on its side, having been fed, and licks its teeth with a loud yawn.

The yawn wasn't the sound I have been waiting for. I led Gavin all the way here, to the animals, because I want to hear the sound that had whispered out of my crystal ball hours ago. A roadie hoses down an elephant. The joyful hosing of water isn't the sound either, but as Gavin's irises grow wider, drinking me in, I know the sound is coming.

A shiver speeds up my arms.

Mulani whinnies again in the rickety corral. Alfred drags a metal can of manure across the hard ground. At the sound of the scrape, I catch my breath. Gavin reaches for me.

CHAPTER FOURTEEN

Only once have I experienced a big top act.

When I first came to the circus, I had no idea what it was, or what was expected of me as one of the acts, so I slipped into the big top during a performance to observe. Men with painted faces and silly clothes zipped around on tiny, motorized bikes making fools of themselves, but high above the rings, a woman in a shimmering leotard swung from a trapeze as if she were made of glittering air.

As she glided up to toward the peak of the tent, I took a breath so swiftly, it lodged in my throat. I couldn't swallow. The woman let go of the bar and somersaulted through the air. I couldn't breathe. Her partner caught her with his muscled arms, and the air rushed out of me. I was dizzy with the thrill of their grace and the way the two glittered like stars above our heads.

Gavin pulls me to him, one hand at my waist and one cradling my neck. Our faces are so close I can feel the heat from his skin. The tiny ripple of excitement rolls through my stomach, growing into a broad wave until it crashes over me. I slide my fingertips down the length of Gavin's arm. He tightens his grip on my waist.

Our lips meet.

This kiss is just like watching the couple on the trapeze. Terrifying. Mesmerizing. Impossible. I'm breathless, as my heart blasts against my ribs.

I break away gently from his kiss.

"Who *are* you?" he whispers.

Looking into his eyes is like looking into a reflection that goes on forever. "Elara—"

"Not your name ... *you*," he explains helplessly. "I've never fallen in love with a girl I just met. I don't believe in it, but here I am, with you. I don't know anything about you, but I want to know everything. I can't stop thinking about you. How are you doing this to me?"

I tip my head to the side and smile, but the guilt embeds itself in my heart. The enchantment is what's doing it to him. I'd love to believe it's purely me, but without the potion, chances are that we would stumble through awkward conversation, he'd ask how he could get ahold of me when I leave town, and then forget about me when I did.

"What do you think I'm doing to you?" I ask, wishing I didn't have to blink, so I wouldn't miss even one glimpse of him. That's the enchantment working, but it's hard to enjoy it, knowing he's confused and might be fighting it.

"I can't ... I have..." he begins, but doesn't finish. His stutter is his sensible self, struggling to surface, trying to make a stand. The enchantment is calling from so deeply inside him, he is probably translating it very close to what it actually is: a calling that will take him away from everything he knows and everything he has.

He reaches for me again, but kisses me hard this time, as if it hurts him to do it.

We're both breathless when he lets go.

I try to remind myself that enchantments have their purpose. They are intense and maybe not made for our situation, but they are a necessity in the gypsy community. Expecting to find a soul mate in the two or three mate choices, especially when we've all known each other since birth, is unrealistic. But with a solid enchantment potion, the problem of living happily-ever-after is solved.

But Gavin isn't a gypsy, and it's not fair that he had no idea what to expect when I gave him a swig of the potion from my flask. The enchantment washed over him so swiftly, I can imagine he was a little frightened by it, maybe even fighting the sensation at first, which only intensifies the enchantment's potency.

Gavin might have *liked* me before, but now, the enchantment will stir his brains, reprioritizing me so that he is willing to kill whole armies to protect me, to be with me, to have me. He hasn't been able to tear his gaze away from me. He stares at the dark fringe of my lower eyelashes, the slope of my nose, my lips and then cycles back through them again.

And I understand it completely, because I'm doing the same to him. I could stay here for days, without food, or water, or air. Just him.

The difference is, I know what's happening.

His next kiss is soft and relentless. I like to think I can distinguish his resolve as it melts away on my lips, but the truth is, I can't be sure.

All I can do is assure myself that he is *the one.* That I'm doing the right thing. That the enchantment would be his choice, if he had one.

I have to give him a choice—

"Do you want to go anywhere?" I ask. "A coffee shop? A park?"

"I want to go wherever you go," he pledges in a whisper. "I want to be with you, Elara...forever."

That was the answer I wanted. Wasn't it? I let myself believe forever will really be this easy for us.

CHAPTER FIFTEEN

M y bones protest as I sit up in my chair. I barely slept after the date with Gavin and here I am awake before dawn.

He took the girl of his dreams walking. All we did was take a walk, stare into each other's eyes, and share a few heated kisses, but by the end of our date, he confided his resolve to go to the ends of the earth for me at least a dozen times. I wish I could shake the clinging doubt.

It seemed real. It felt real. I almost believe he truly means it.

I felt the same as him, but now, with the true, younger me folded down inside Edeva's old body, I feel like a deflated *jack in the box* toy. I thought that reverting back to my older self would give me some relief, but it turned out to be a bigger struggle than I'd anticipated. Not because of the aches and pains that come with putting on the Edeva skin, but because it means I cannot be with Gavin.

The enchantment makes me want to spend every second, being me, *Elara,* with Gavin.

There is a hollowness in Edeva that aches to my core.

I believe Gavin must feel the same emptiness. If so, he's probably waiting outside my wagon door right now.

The thrill of it whistles through me, but when I open the door and step out, into the darkness, he's not here.

Instead, the carnival sleeps all around me, except the stray yowl from one of the animals and the hum of the protective, mobile lights overhead.

I start fire, hang my pot over it, and take out my bag of *gorne.* From the corner of my eye, I see a sharp, orange streak of a star shoots across the sky.

My old eyes rivet to the crackling star. Instead of falling toward the horizon, the star crests from the left of the sky to the right. It finally comes to a halt like a spitting flame, dark as the burnt innards of a pumpkin. I hope the color stabilizes, but it continues to deepen instead, turning a hideous shade of crimson.

I drop the bag of *gorne.* The grain cascades over my shoes.

Goose bumps race up my wrinkled arms. Whether or not I'm ready to execute the final parts of my plan doesn't matter anymore. The blazing, orange star means the original *Scorched Soul* has not only learned of my mission, but knows I am trying to eradicate him, just as he is trying to destroy me.

If he finds me before I reach my destination, the *Scorched Soul* will snuff me out without a second thought. My mission, my life, will have been for nothing.

There is no more time. I must collect everything I can in this little town as quickly as possible. My old heart is overwhelmed by its own beat. Even if I can collect an army, nothing is guaranteed. Everything I do may be for nothing anyway.

"Miss Edeva?" Gavin's voice cuts through the darkness as he steps from the shadows. "I didn't mean to startle you, but I need to speak with your granddaughter."

My hollowness intensifies. The need to be with me —*Elara*—tortures him too.

But I still have work that must be done. I must have Leonard Drake before I can leave.

Gavin's eyes hang on the back door of my wagon. I step into his line of vision, blocking the door, as a thin vein of fear rushes down my back. I didn't have to collect Gavin, he came willingly, but since he's enchanted to me, we've joined one another. We're as good as the same person now. The spell on the wagon door won't keep him out.

"She went to feed our horse, Mulani," I lie.

Gavin's stare is rooted over my shoulder. "No," he declares in a curious whisper. "I can *feel* her. She's *here*."

"I promise you..." I begin, but he tears past me. My stiff joints don't respond quickly enough to catch him. He bounds up the steps of the wagon and throws open the door, disappearing inside.

I hobble up the steps after him and promptly slam into his back. Gavin stands in the cramped walkway, gaping at the aisle that stretches far longer than the exterior of my wagon could possibly reach.

"Is that an optical illusion? This wagon isn't that long...or big." He points into the distance, toward a back wall we can't even see. On either side, bolts upon bolts of colorful fabric are stacked on the floor and shelves that ascend far too high to be accurate to my wagon's dimensions.

Gavin's wide eyes roll upward to the sky-high ceiling and down the walls again, to the floor. The upper most shelves hold smaller rolls of fabric, since they hold the animals I've collected and could more easily heft up to the high ledges.

"You're not supposed to be in here," I say.

Gavin spots an exposed shoe. "Is that someone's *foot?*"

He reaches out with a hesitant hand, swiftly flipping back the edge of one of the fabric rolls as if it will explode. A woman's leg is exposed, up to the calf.

He stumbles backward, slamming into the opposite side of the aisle.

A groan releases from another roll and Gavin springs back to the center of the walkway. He turns to me, wild-eyed.

"Are all these people dead?"

CHAPTER SIXTEEN

"They're not dead," I say, but my words have no soothing effect.

"You better tell me where Elara is, right now!" He shouts, his wide, wild gaze tumbling over the bolts of wrapped bodies. I am sure that the more he looks, the more the hands and feet and bulbs of heads become obvious.

"Let me explain," I say softly. "I am a *collector*."

His eyes only grew wilder. "Of dead people?"

"I told you, none of them are dead. They're all quite alive and healthy."

"They're not moving and they're wrapped in rugs...*on shelves*!" He stabs a finger at some rolls of fabric.

"They don't need to move, and they are breathing. If you listen, you can hear some of them snore." I turn to one

77

of the rolls, lean down, and speak to it sweetly. "Would you kindly prove to Gavin that you are alive?"

"*Ahhhiiivvve.*" The voice is as wheezy as an accordion from inside the roll and hardly sounds human. Gavin starts at the sound, but he's deep enough in the cabin, he'd have to knock me down to get to the door. I don't know how much longer I can pacify him.

"Where's Elara?" he bellows. "Tell me where she is right now!"

A droplet of terror swizzles down my spine. This isn't the way I wanted to do it.

I knew I'd have to reveal myself, but I hoped to do it when we reached our final destination. Revealing myself now could change everything I've seen in my crystal ball, and it could even change the fact that Gavin is my chosen one, if revealing myself to him is too much for him to handle. He could have a mental breakdown at the sight of it. If the *enchantment* potion hasn't completely swayed him, then there won't be enough to change it after he sees the transformation, and with the *Scorched Soul* closing in, there isn't any more time.

"There's something I have to tell you—" I say.

He takes a deep breath and speaks beneath it, trying to keep the quivers out of his voice, I think. "I don't want to hear anything else out of you, ma'am. Not until I see Elara, and I want to see her right now!"

"Alright," I say. There's nothing I can say to prepare him.

I reach into my pocket, retrieve my sprinkling of constellation-ambiance-comet dust, and raise it over my head. My stiff movements have nothing to do with the workings of Edeva's body, and everything to do with my hesitation. Caught between what might be, and what might not, I give up my inner struggle and open my fist. The burnt, sweet smell of the dust filters through my nostrils, and with one short breath, it coats the back of my throat. I can taste the ambiance. The dust dries on the deepest part of my tongue and I cough.

This has to work. But if it doesn't...

The dust sticks to my skin. Youthful skin spreads outward from the dust, like water drenching a paper napkin. My wrinkles smooth as if I've run them over with a hot iron. The dust on my forehead disintegrates, the milky cataracts dissolving from my eyes. My cheeks regain their beautiful, rosy color. My lips plump. My teeth brighten into the wide smile I aim at Gavin.

Gavin's eyes roll upward. Then backward. They disappear into his head, right before he drops like a pile of rocks at my feet.

CHAPTER SEVENTEEN

G avin isn't out for more than a few seconds, but when he comes to, he jumps to his feet. He handled the rolled bodies, but this is the tipping point. It's too much for him.

I throw my hands up in front of me. "Listen to me first—"

"What did you do to Elara? What are you?" A swirl of fury churns in his gaze. The enchantment should've made him incapable of expressing anger toward me, but he doesn't seem to recognize me as me right now. I move a step backward as he takes a menacing stride toward me.

There are too few options.

I might be able to charm him, so he rolls himself up on a shelf and slumbers until we get where we need to be.

But, I won't know until he awakens in our new life, whether or not the enchantment has been broken from the startling revelation of my dual form.

I can't risk losing him.

There's only one other choice.

"Intruder," I whisper.

The wagon responds with a sonic *boom* that rattles through the interior of the cabin. The vibration shakes the shelves, quivering the bolts of fabric upon them, but I only feel the sound as it shivers up through the floorboards into my legs.

My gypsy ears can't detect the frequency, calibrated to stun human beings, and the noise is isolated to the wagon's interior, so that even if someone was leaning up against the exterior, they wouldn't hear a thing. The bolts of fabric shudder again and Gavin drops in his tracks.

The cabin is silent.

Gavin's body sprawls across the floor, the only movement, a tranquilized blink of his eyes.

I ease myself down to sit beside Gavin, gathered his head in my lap. "You don't understand what I'm doing, and I have to be able to explain."

The sedated blink continues as I run my fingers through his hair. I remain here, beneath the sagging purple fabric of one of the shelved rolls, humming songs my mother once hummed to me, until his eyelids quiver.

When his field of vision narrows enough to find me, it's clear that he doesn't remember what just happened. An easy grin spreads over his lips. The good news: he is still enchanted.

But then, his lips twitch. He sits up so quickly, we bump heads.

We both groan and sit back against the fabric bolts on either side of the aisle, rubbing our skulls.

He blinks hard now, studying me. "What are you?" he asks.

"A gypsy," I say, "from the Mercury clan."

"No...I mean, you were an old woman!"

"We are both things. Sometimes, we are all things."

"*We*, who? Who are you talking about? I'm none of those things!" He reaches back, his arm across the edge of a shelf to propel himself to his feet, but when he feels the fabric, he winces and snatches back his hand.

"We, meaning each of us." I try to calm him with my tone. I'm not sure it's working. "You are *only* young right now because you haven't reached old age yet. When you become old, you will find that your youth is still within you and—"

"I *saw* you *change*!" His laughter is more of a bark than an expression of joy. "I've got to be losing my mind!"

"You're not," I soothe. "It's just a lot to take in, if it's never been explained to you before."

82

He considers it a moment, and then slides back down to the floor, pulling his knees up and cradling his head in his hands. "Why don't I want to leave? This is crazy. You're crazy, this whole thing is crazy, and all I want to do is stay here with you."

I scoot closer. "We chose each other."

"What are you talking about?" he moans.

"I chose you to come with me," I say. He shakes his head, but I reach out and put my hand on his. I am delighted when he doesn't push me away. "I am a collector, Gavin, and I am gathering people who have dreamed of being magical. People who desire to make a difference in the world, and people who dream of new lives. I'm giving all of them everything they've ever wanted."

He remains silent, but I think he's actually listening. "Where?"

I'm elated with even his faint utterance of interest. "You're asking, where we are going? We're going to the foothills of Mount Eellyis. Ever heard of it?"

He shakes his head, but I already knew the answer.

There's no way he could have heard of it. I don't know that he can handle the rest—that this barren place is a pocket dimension— a tiny dimension of empty space, which is stitched over the top of the same space in his home dimension. From the Dimensional Column, the pocket isn't easily detected. Within the dimension itself, the fog of the *vias* obscures the pathway which still connects the two dimensions. Travelers in Gavin's dimension may travel, completely unaware, beneath the entire pocket, or, if they encounter the edge of the *vias,* where the dimensions actually connect, travelers would likely reroute around the murky fog. I may even spell the *vias* to further deter intruders and avoid them being lost in the *vias* forever, or worse, stumbling upon us.

"We're going to build a village where we can rehabilitate *scorched souls*. I need witches and warlocks. Lots of them. That's who all these people are." I motion to the piles of fabric bolts. "But you ... you are here because you are much more. You are meant to be mine, and you are meant to be a great *witch doctor*—"

He stands up first. Then, he paces the floor, back and forth, back and forth, each time inching a bit closer to the door. I don't bother to tell him the door won't open for him. Since he was declared an intruder, I have to absolve him with a kiss before he can come and go freely again. Still, he inches closer to the door. I don't believe he'll actually open it, not with the enchantment pumping desire for me through his veins.

When he reaches for the door, my magic makes it there only seconds before he turns the knob. I open my palm and pull it back, overriding the absolution for this one escape. He won't be able to come back in without my consent, but I have to let him leave if that is what he truly wants.

That is the curse of loving someone.

Accepting their will. Letting them go.

He flings the door open, his body filling the threshold before he rushes down the steps. I watch him disappear, hoping he'll turn back, but he doesn't.

The orange star crackles in the sky he leaves behind.

CHAPTER EIGHTEEN

The crystal ball is maddeningly fogged. I've been antsy all day, reading fortunes that have absolutely no use to me, impatiently waiting for Leonard Drake to come, but mostly yearning for Gavin to return.

The orange star has gained attention. It's been reported on the news, noted with great concern by religious groups, and investigated by environmentalists who can make nothing of it.

Two camps seem to have emerged in the small metric I observe at the fairgrounds. The first camp panics over the blazing star that doesn't disappear with the night, and the second camp blatantly ignores it. Either way, all of the attention only worsens my circumstances. The *scorched soul* is hunting for me and will continue to search until he finds me.

If it weren't for my aching desire to have Gavin Faye as mine, I think I'd just abandon Drake altogether. As it is, I only justify the danger of waiting.

I read the fortune of a man who wanted to win the lottery and never will; a teen boy who wants to be married to a girl who is already picking out rings; a woman involved in an affair and who wanted to know, but not really, the dire outcome. I read a woman who designs computer programs, and was happy to tell her how famous she will be.

But even in the joy of good fortune, I hurry through the readings, and in between, I scour the depths of the crystal ball to find Gavin. For the first time in the length of my existence, my own fortune seems as tumbled in the great cauldron of the future as any of my customers who pay in tickets.

By dusk, I am exhausted, and by the time the midway thins, I'm feeling that my crystal ball has turned against me. That is, until Leonard Drake appears like an apparition at midnight. Then, I'm sure of it.

Drake stands in the doorway of my tent, cracking his knuckles. The beaded partition drips silently over the high bulbs of his shoulders. His hair is wet with a sheen of sweat. It's not shocking, since he's resisted the call of his dreams for days now.

"I've come to have my fortune read," he says.

I don't even answer. I immediately set about charming his mind, and then, send him walking across the fairgrounds to my wagon, with two of my shawl disks pinned to his chest for entry.

As soon as he's gone, I drop onto my chair. I can't stall any longer. My justification for sticking around Lake Linden is now on his way to my wagon. I can't delay this mission any longer.

I take one more sorrowful glance into my crystal ball, searching for Gavin. His face appears, filling the glass, stretching his temples. I grimace into the glass, stroking the cool edges, trying to adjust the vision.

"Hello, Elara," Gavin says from the tent opening.

I startle backward in my chair. Gavin wasn't in the ball at all. He's standing in the opening of my tent, the beads draped over his shoulders. A warning would've been nice.

"I can't stay away, but it doesn't mean I'll stay forever either." His jaw tenses. "Everything about this is wrong. You're a stranger and it's crazy for me to just up and leave with you out of the blue. I have responsibilities. People count on me."

"And even more will, in the place we're going. The hole you leave behind here will fill in," I promise. "If you worry about your past, I can erase you from this place and these people, so no one will ever realize you were here at all."

"No, I don't want them to forget me."

"Alright. They can sorrow, if you prefer it. They will believe you died."

He nods, brow furrowed, his struggle with what I'm offering— and what he wants—visible.

"I'd like to see Elara now."

I reach into my pocket, gathering a handful of transformative dust in my palm, and raise it over my head. "Are you sure you want to watch?" I ask.

"I'm not going to run away again," he whispers.

I let the dust cascade over my skin. I'm relieved to shed Edeva's skin and finish with a deep breath and smile at Gavin.

I go around the table and without hesitation, I move in close and kiss him. Deeply. His hands run up over my shoulders and into my hair. His kiss is oxygen.

He draws back with a smile, but his gaze trips over my shoulder.

"Is that supposed to happen?" he asks, pointing behind me. I turn to see the interior of my crystal ball glow a blistering, red.

CHAPTER NINETEEN

The crystal ball is easier for me to juggle in my own, youthful arms. Gavin follows me out of the tent, but we stop just outside the opening, staring up at a second star shooting across the sky as if someone has fired a flare gun. Seething red, its path arches like a rainbow and then stops abruptly beside the first star that's been hovering above the midway like a burning flower stuck in a deathly lapel.

Fear burns just as bright in the pit of my stomach.

A third star of warning shoots out from behind the other two and all three burn out in a sudden fizz, leaving a small, charred triangle in the otherwise clear sky. We are left in darkness, the fairground flood lights dim at a distance from my tent. The streaks of the three stars hang overhead like an open mouth.

I catch my breath.

Gavin turns to me. "What did that mean?"

"We have to leave. Tonight. Now," I say. The hair at the back of my neck itches and won't lie down.

The beads of my tent door give a trill.

"Here it is!" a girl shrieks as she drags a boy around the edge of my tent. "Let's get our fortunes read!"

"Sorry, this show is closed. The fortune teller stepped out for the night!" I say.

The girl pushes out her lower lip. "But the circus is still open and we got tickets!"

"You're the fortune teller! You've got the ball, so give us our fortune!" The boy motions to the crystal ball in the crook of my elbow and thrust a small pile of tickets into my free hand.

I gasp, the surge of *scorching* racing up my arm on contact.

Gavin steps between the boy and me. "The lady said the tent is closed."

"No, it's okay. I'll do this last one," I say, moving out from behind him. The last place the love of my life needs to be is between me and this boy. Gavin has no idea how helpless he'd be against one of the *scorched*. "Please," I say to the young couple, "come in."

Gavin cocks his head, puzzled. I return as easy a smile as I can manage. There's no time to explain why I can't just leave a *scorched soul* behind.

"You said we have to go!" Gavin whispers as he takes my hand and gives me a brief tug away from the tent.

I shake loose. I can't leave yet. I've come to heal the *scorched,* and leaving any of them behind, especially those who present themselves so clearly, only allows for the infection to spread further.

"I have to do this first," I tell him. "Just trust me, okay? Go find the roadie named Alfred. Ask him to hook up Mulani, and if he asks why, tell him the ringmaster asked me to do a jaunt around town to beef up the crowds."

"Alright," Gavin says, but he turns away slowly, still scrutinizing me from over his shoulder as he leaves.

I don't know if our bond is strong enough yet for him to feel what's pulsing through me as I go into the tent—a mixture of fear, bravery, terror, and will. I hope he can't, or he'll be back before I can do what I must.

The crystal storms inside as I stride into the tent and set it on the pedestal. I'm not sure how well this will go with the two of them here.

"Aren't you going to tell us anything?" the boy snaps when I don't speak. He stands beside the girl, who is seated in the chair.

"You need help," I say, "and I'm waiting to find out how I can give it to you."

"*I* need help?" The boy laughs. "She's the one who stole the dope!"

"You weren't supposed to say!" The girl squeals. Her

amusement tells me she's already consumed whatever she stole. "Let her tell it! Maybe she meant help because you've been so *boo-face* lately," the girl says. "Is that what you were talking about? His depression?"

Within the ball, I see the girl's truth first. She's not *scorched,* she's high.

The fog of my own unsure future suddenly scuttles over the ball. Now we're getting somewhere. I wait to see the best way of handling the boy—which is to say, the dimension in which I do it best—but as I continue to squint, a smudge emerges from the center of the crystal.

"What are you looking at?" the boy asks, leaning forward from his side of the table.

I gasp as the slick head of an eel becomes clear. The thing splays open its mouth and bears the silver tines of its fangs at me, before diving straight at my heart. I throw my hands in front of me on impulse, and nearly knock the ball from the pedestal. The beast's head clanks against the inside of the ball, the sound of its shriek filling the tent.

I am on my feet, staggering backward, as my eyes meet those of the boy.

His smile is deadly.

"You *know* you're blackened," I breathe. "You know what you are!"

"I didn't come for a stupid fortune, I came for *you.*"

"He's magical," The girl yells from the chair as the boy stalks around the table. I reach into my pocket, feeling around for anything that will help. My hand closes on a fistful of the transformative dust, the biggest fistful I can manage to grasp.

"Aren't you going to run?" He reaches for me and I hurl the dust on him.

He shouts, stumbling backward, his hand on the flimsy table.

"What did you do to him?" the girl shrieks a laugh, clapping as if this was the first act of a play, instead of the treacherous interlude it is.

I snatch up my crystal ball just as the plywood table top flips off the barrel beneath it. The boy, shrinking in stature, falls behind the table top as the girl continues to shriek. He has transformed to a very little boy, maybe four years old or so, drowning in oversized clothing. Despite his size, he lunges for me and I throw another half-handful of dust on him.

The girl stands, laughing hysterically, completely unaware of the real danger she is in. She may not be *scorched* yet, but the boy's influence got her here.

Depression is one of the first signs. Crimes and misconduct of all sorts comes next. Murder, or suicide, comes after that. Then, after death, the *scorched soul* wanders in misery and passes the infection to whomever they can. That is the final stage and it goes on forever, unless the soul is rehabilitated.

Humans have no idea of the depths to which the misery of *scorching* can plunge them.

If the boy had succeeded in killing me, he would've considered it a triumph. If I kill him now, he'll infect the girl.

It occurs to me, that's why he's brought her.

To win.

But if I can get him to my wagon, I win. He won't expect that. The *scorched* never expect grace.

The girl continues to laugh hysterically, pointing at the boy. He's shrunken down to an infant.

My crystal ball in one arm, I scoop up the infant boy in the other and duck behind the partition, racing through the coil of the tent, leaving the girl's laughter behind.

Breaking out of the coiled wall and into the dark night, the infant boy clamps onto my bicep. His toothless gums pinch and will leave a bruise, but no matter how he tries, he doesn't break the skin. I race through the fairground shadows toward my wagon.

CHAPTER TWENTY

Mulani squeals as I sprint toward the wagon. Gavin is seated on the driver's bench.

"What is that?" he shouts down to me when he spots the baby latched to my arm.

"A customer," I say as I pull the infant loose. The baby lets out one frustrated cry before I charm him. I hurry around the wagon and the back door of the wagon swings open as I rifle up the steps. Inside, I deposit the baby between two rolls of fabric containing motherly women. It's the best I can do.

My arm aches from carrying the crystal ball, but I hang onto it as I climb the back of the wagon.

Overhead, a blood red star fires across the sky, pulsing as if the heavens were ablaze. Mulani's ears prick back.

"What does *that* mean?" Gavin asks, stabbing a finger in the direction of the warning star.

My entire body goes cold as I scramble across the top of the wagon and into the driver's seat beside him. I push my crystal ball into his hands and grab Mulani's reins.

"HYAH!" I shout, bringing down the reins with a hard snap. Mulani surges forward, the wheels hurling clumps of grass in the air.

Gavin falls backward against the back of the bench. Once he regains his balance, he twists on the seat to scan the dusty shadows we're leaving behind.

"Is someone chasing us?" he asks.

"Something will be," I say.

"Something? What do you mean, *something*?"

"That star up there means the *scorched soul* is closing in. We're out of time!" I push the reins at Gavin and take the crystal ball back.

"I don't know how to drive a horse!" he shouts.

"It's just like driving a bike!" I stand, rocking on my feet.

"Sit down!" He switches the reins into one hand and tries to grab at me with the other, but Mulani surges forward, forcing Gavin to grip the reins tightly in both fists again. "You're going to fall off and I'm going to run you over!"

"I know what I'm doing!" I yell back. "Trust me!"

The wagon lurches and Gavin lets out a scream as I

stagger, struggling to keep my footing. Holding the crystal ball in both hands, I lob it over Mulani's head with every bit of strength I have. The ball flies ahead of the wagon as if it is propelling itself. It falls and rolls across the ground, exploding with a burst of *vias* smoke.

A foggy-edged mirage of foothills, and a great mountain rising up beyond them, appears ahead of us. Gavin shouts as Mulani leaps into the plume, the wagon jerking upward as it bursts through the fog.

CHAPTER TWENTY-ONE

"Is this part of the carnival? Where are we?" Gavin's voice is high and stringy as he grips the wagon bench and peers all around us with wide eyes. He obviously knows his home town well enough to know we're not there any longer.

There is nothing to see but a flat carpet of bluegrass, stretching for miles and miles, beneath a clear blue sky. At the furthest most edges, in every direction, a barrier of fog mingles among high reaching trees that sport tangled trunks. The trees are topped with dense shower caps of leaves and oddly-long branches. Some of the limbs hang, laced at the bottoms like a mother cradling a child, while others are wrapped around surrounding trees as if they are offering one another support and friendship.

Otherwise, the ground between us and the trees is empty and waiting. Ready for the village we've come to construct.

"We escaped." I'm still breathless.

"Escaped what?" he asks.

"The *Scorched Soul.* The original, I think." Mulani slows from a canter to a walk. "Don't worry, no one is going to find us here."

Gavin twists on the bench, looking in one direction, then slowly turns and looks in the other, but there is no change in the landscape no matter where I look.

"Where are we? This isn't Lake Linden." His Adam's apple jumps as he swallows.

"It's exactly what I asked for. This is a replica of your world, sewn like a pocket on top of your dimension."

He ignores that I don't claim his world since he's busy squinting at the milky boundaries in the distance. "Is that *fog?*"

"It's called a *vias.* It separates this pocket from the real dimension, so that it obscures this space from the outside, but we can travel to the outer world as necessary."

"What are you talking about?" He leans away from me on the bench, his eyes still wide with shock. "We were just at the carnival. Is this part of the carnival?"

"No. It's a pocket—"

"Stop saying that," he snaps. "This isn't right. We have to go back."

"We can't," I tell him solidly. "This is what we've come for, Gavin. This is the beginning of the new life I told you about. This pocket was a gift, so we could create a village that will heal the scorched."

"A gift to heal the scorched," he repeats in a monotone. "Who gives a gift like that?"

"Joy does," I tell him with a grin, but as I reach for his hand, but Gavin yanks it away.

He runs a shaky hand through his hair. "This is crazy...this whole thing is crazy...I think you're crazy."

I expected him to be shocked, but he's not snapping out of it.

"This is a fresh start for all of us," I say softly.

"Who are you talking about?" He twists on the bench again, glimpsing each direction as if he expects to find a crowd waiting in the distance.

"You know some of the others," I say. I'm not certain how to make this introduction any less jarring, but I am not sure there will ever be a way to do it. I shimmy down from the bench, my feet landing hard on the dirt. "Well, come on," I say and it takes Gavin moment before he jumps down too. He stays a short distance from me, but follows me to the back porch of the wagon.

I bang the arch with my elbow, clanging the disks of my shawl, and the door springs open. I walk inside, but Gavin stays on the stoop.

"Come in," I coax. "I need your help. It was hard

enough to get each of them in here, but I'm not dragging them out by myself, even if I'm not an old woman anymore. You're plenty strong," I say, taking a long, appreciative look at his biceps. "Help me. It will be a lot easier if you grab their feet."

CHAPTER TWENTY-TWO

"There are people in there?" The color drains from Gavin's face as he spots a foot sticking out of one of the fabric rolls. He studies the other rolls, not budging from his station outside the door. "Are they all...dead?"

I scoff. "Of course not. They're only suspended."

"They're not moving! And they're wrapped in rugs!"

"It was too long of a journey to have them all mulling around in here, eating my food and asking questions."

"Where did they all come from?" His vocal cords must be stretched to breaking. His voice disappears at points.

"Everywhere." I shrug. "I've travelled across the country and brought them from everywhere."

"Kidnapped?"

"Collected," I correct. "Are you going to come in and help me?"

"No." He looks to the right, then the left, probably contemplating where he could possibly run to, but there's nowhere to go.

"If you go into the *vias,* that fog, you'll be lost until I come to find you with my gypsy glass. It would take a lot of time that we could spend in much better ways."

He scoffs. "Like burying bodies?"

"We can't bury the living," I tell him. This conversation makes me wary. Now that we are here, we have an enormous amount of work to do, and I can tell how valuable it is that I shed the old woman disguise because I'm going to have to heft these bodies out of the wagon by myself.

I throw my shawl over my shoulders. The discs at the edge of the covering grumble, sliding together with effort, as I take hold of one of the smaller fabric rolls and drag the body by the foot onto the wagon stoop. Gavin jumps down, out of the way. This is doing nothing for his anxiety, but I can't wake any of them up inside the wagon. Sometimes they come out of suspension with a rush of energy that could hurt the others or destroy my wagon.

"Please?" I say to Gavin, motioning for him to get the shoulders at the other end, but he only shakes his head. "For goodness sakes...fine...I'll do it myself."

I grunt as I pull the body down the three stairs, the roll of fabric cushioning the head, although it still thumps against the steps. I'm panting once the body is on the ground and rolled safely away from the wagon stoop. I unroll the body from the fabric and Gavin's face drains to an even paler gray.

"That's Leonard Drake," he says. "I knew him."

"You still do. I told you, he's not dead! Just watch!"

I grip the edge of the shawl and hold it up in front of me. Not one disk touches. They hang straight down, like a row of slumbering, silver bats.

"Wake him," I whisper as I drag my finger down the row, swinging the disks so they create a chime as soft and appealing as the call of any siren. The song hails the man back to consciousness, but he awakens in a panic.

"What...what happened?" Eyes wide and gulping for air, he jumps to his feet and stumbles backward, his gaze lashing between Gavin and me. "What did you do to me, Faye?"

Gavin puts up his hands. "I didn't do any—"

"*She* did it then?" Leonard Drake spears a finger at me. "Yes, that's right. I heard you! Who are you?" He turns back on Gavin. "How do you know her?

"I..." Gavin's voice drains away. When he glimpses me, I see his faith in everything I've said, or will say, disappearing too.

I focus completely on Leonard Drake and he narrows his eyes on me in return. "I've brought you here to give you everything you've been wanting."

"How *in the hills* could you presume to know what I want?"

"You have worked so hard," I begin gently, remembering the desperate desires I felt in his collected dreams. Such a simple thing to say, and yet, the furrows of his brow soften. "This world needs your diligence. I will give you a career so successful and fulfilling that you will never doubt what I know about you—that you are brilliant and well-thought, strong, and capable. I know you are shackled in a situation that you've been looking to escape. You only need a fresh start and the chance to prove yourself."

"Now, wait a minute." Gavin says. "He's got a wife and they've got a baby coming! Is his wife here, or are you saying he should just leave them behind?"

A hesitant grin wavers onto Leonard Drake's lips. The latter is exactly what he wants, but he'll never admit it. That desire was lodged carefully beneath all the other dreams Drake entertains.

"I promised everyone I brought the same thing I promised you. A new life," I say.

Gavin grips his forehead. "I didn't leave behind a pregnant wife! I thought I could be on board here, but this...this is too much!"

And now it's going way too far. Gavin shoulders are squared and tight, his palm slides back, pulling his hairline. Drake breaks out in a sweat, maybe from guilt, but most likely because his greatest desire is on the verge of slipping away.

"Maybe it's none of your business, Faye," Leonard Drake growls. "Maybe she's joining me at a later date."

Gavin turns on him. "Maybe? I would think if it was my wife who was carrying my first born, I'd be a little more sure of what the plans are!"

Embroiled in the heated debate, I take the opportunity to retrieve the long-necked bottle from inside the wagon. Round as a bowling ball at the bottom, a ball of cork plugs the fluted neck. The wine inside is blacker than old blood. I scoop up the cup and bowl I use for my meals and hold the bulbous bottle in the crook of my arm, the liquid sloshing so much, it halts Gavin and Drake's argument the moment I approach with it.

"We could all use a breather," I say. "Anyone care for a drink?"

CHAPTER TWENTY-THREE

"You need to take us back to Lake Linden," Gavin says.

My hope stumbles. The enchantment wasn't enough. I will have to use the *shadow wine* I acquired.

"I'll take the drink," Leonard Drake reaches for the cup. Grateful, I hand it over, along with the bowl. I should've given them the wine immediately, but there wasn't any opportunity.

"Unfortunately, all I have is the cup and the bowl," I say as I fill each of them.

Drake hands the bowl to Gavin and the cup to me, then reaches for the bottle for himself. "I can drink from the bottle, if you will excuse my manners."

"Of course," I say, handing it over. "No excuse necessary, Leonard. We're all friends now, aren't we?"

Leonard Drake scoffs with a tolerant grin.

Gavin looks off into the distance toward the cloudy *vias*. He's probably considering if escape is even possible. Luckily, I have a remedy for his anxiety. All of his residual concerns will be over in a few moments.

Drake holds up the bottle, considering the dark liquid within. "What kind of wine is this? It's the darkest I've seen. Blackberry? Malbec, or maybe saperavi grapes?"

"A mixture," I say with a wry smile as I raise my cup. Better that they don't know the mixture will erase their failures and delicately reconstruct their memories so their new lives, here, with me, will be logic and comfortable to them. Still, I make my toast appropriate to the moment. "Here's to returning to Lake Linden!"

Gavin clinks the bowl to my cup with a suspicious scowl, and Leonard Drake softly tinks my cup with the side of the bottle. I pretend my drink, though I don't tip my cup enough for the wine to touch my lips. Drake takes a long, full drink, a bubble rising to the bottom of the upended bottle as he does. Gavin, however, takes his drink and wipes his mouth on his sleeve.

The sight is incredibly satisfying, since it will only take a few moments before Leonard Drake and Gavin Faye forget their interests in Lake Linden all together and connect with the eagerness of their desires to begin the new lives I promised, here, in this pocket dimension.

Drake takes a second, long swallow. I reach up and push the bottle down, cutting him off. I can't have him forgetting his entire reason for being.

Gavin blinks at me as if there's something caught in his eye. He moves his gaze to the wagon, to Leonard Drake, to the tree line and the *vias* fog, then back to me.

"I'm supposed to be here, right?" Gavin asks.

"Yes, you are," I tell him.

"With you," he adds as if he's not sure whether I might slap him for assuming it.

I smile. "Yes, with me."

"Good...because I think I'm in love with you." The intensity of his gaze knocks the wind out of me.

"You are." I whisper. He seems so genuine. Has to be. The enchantment must've only needed a little extra boost from the *shadow wine* to really take effect and I must've needed him to look at me like he is now, to feel the power of the enchantment as it reaches into my soul and steals my heart.

"I'm looking for the love of my life," Leonard Drake pipes up. We both turn to look at him. "Where is she?"

He's not asking for the wife he left behind. He's talking about the new love of his life that comes with this new world.

"In the back of the wagon, somewhere," I tell him. "We

have to wake everyone so we can toast to our new lives here."

"Yes, let's do that." Drake swivels his head, scanning the landscape with a drunk grin. "Where are we?"

I follow his gaze to the tree line. "Leaf Scape," I say.

He shrugs. "Never heard of it, but then again, why would I, when there's nothing here?"

"*We're* here," Gavin says. I ignore the slight frown that pulls the edges of his lips down. The wine must need a bit longer to take full effect.

CHAPTER TWENTY-FOUR

L eonard Drake has another characteristic that drives him. We finish unrolling all the bodies and while Gavin and I take a break on the grass, Drake picks through the slumbering figures, looking for a suitable wife.

"You're very superficial," Gavin muses as he reclines beside me and plays with my fingers.

"I'm searching for the woman I will love the rest of my life," Drake says. "No one wants to look at a stern face over their supper every night."

"You know," Gavin drawls, "you're trying to pick a peach, but the way you're going about it, you might still get a pickle."

"I know what appeals to me," Drake says with a sour glimpse at my fingers laced between Gavin's. He swings his gaze away like a blade. "Luckily, I have excellent intuition and the choices I make are none of your business."

"Don't you want to wait until they wake and you can talk to them?"

Drake rolls his shoulders, but continues his search. "The right one will speak to me all the same."

"Spoken like a true woman," Gavin chides, but Drake only waves him off.

"There are at least one hundred women here," I tell Gavin. "It's going to take him a while."

We stretch out on the grass, gazing at the clouds drifting lazily across the starless sky. There is so much work to do. Waking all of them, spelling them and training them to use their new magic, matching them all to spouses who most of them have never met before, but will accept with a bit of enchantment potion. The rehabilitative vortex should already be here somewhere, but I can only release the scorched souls into it once the training is complete.

I can't forget about Zelda's husband and the young man who I transformed into an infant. The small child lying in the grass appears peacefully asleep, even if the entire scene of bodies strewn everywhere seems a bit macabre. I must separate the *scorched soul* from the body, so we'll need to erect a storage house to store the bodies until the souls are rehabilitated and can return to them.

And the animals. I've brought all sorts, some for food, and some that will become *notas,* feeding the magic and healing energy of the witches and warlocks. I hope the tiny green and blue humming birds aren't lost in the grass. There are pigs and goats, and even cows that were horrible to extract from the wagon. There are no roosters or hens, but there are eggs, hidden away in a cushioned bag, to be incubated at a much later date. I can't handle the sight of them. As for the spiders and insects, they too are stored in a silk bag.

I yawn, thinking of all the work ahead of us.

"I think I'm going to wake the animals first," I ponder aloud.

"Where are we going to put them?" Gavin asks, looking around again. We'll need a barn. There is only grass and lines of trees so far, and the hulking mountain that rises up from our left. When Gavin sees it, he gives it a long stare. "Was that here before? I don't remember a mountain being there. I couldn't have missed a whole mountain."

The things we need for our village will continue to appear, but the human conception of reality is so delicate, I won't crowd Gavin's processing with those.

"It was here." I tell him. "There's a lake here some-where too, but we're going to have to build our dwellings."

Gavin gapes. "Elara, I don't know how to build houses!"

"That's not your job. I've brought architects and builders for that. I'm very prepared."

"We'll need tools."

"They're in the wagon's lower level."

"Wheel barrows? Ladders? Tractors? Diggers? Scaffolding? You've got that?"

"If I don't, I'm sure everything we need is here somewhere. We'll find it."

"It's unbelievable that your little wagon fit all these people and now you're telling me it has a lower level too? And that we'll just *happen* to *find* whatever we need to build a whole village here?"

"It's absolutely unbelievable," I say, "but that's magic for you."

He flashes me a sheepish grin. "Sure it is."

"You believe in magic," I say softly. "I know you do."

"A certain kind of magic," he says, squeezing my hand.

If it's genuine, that would be enough for me. "You're going to be an incredible witch doctor."

"About that," he says, reaching up to scrub the hair above his ear. "If you thought I'm a doctor, I'm not. And whatever a *witch doctor* is, it sounds like it belongs in Halloween land."

"I knew you weren't a doctor, but I also know that you are capable of greatness, and you've always wanted a worthy and useful position in life. I will train you for it myself. You will be the only witch doctor in the village, and all the witches and warlocks will depend on you."

"How many people are you talking about? Everyone

here?" he asks. His tone is less eager than it is appre-
hensive.

I soften my tone to soothe him. "They won't all be
needing care at any one time. You'll care for them and their
children—"

"You want me to do this alone?"

"I'm going to help you." I cinch my upper lip between
my teeth. I have to tread carefully. "And our child will
help too."

He perks. "Child?"

I'm surprised at the grin that spreads over his lips.

"We're going to have kids?"

"Let's start with one." I nibble my lip again.

"I don't understand it," he says with a chuckle. "I am
looking forward to a life with you here, but I don't know
why I don't miss home at all."

I smooth some hair at his temple. "This is our home."

"Yeah," he muses, "but I would've thought I'd miss my
family. It feels like I never will."

I debate telling him about the Grandmother Trees, or
the Grandfather Rocks. How the tiny pebbles in Lake
Tinneret and the pollination from the trees hold the vibrations of mothers, fathers, and siblings who eventually
become the Grandmothers and the Grandfathers.

Maybe I'll explain all of that some other time, when
our home isn't so new and our mission here hasn't just
begun. I know I don't have forever, but I have some, and

it's not in my game plan to break any fragile human ideologies today.

"I found her!" Leonard Drake calls out. "I found my beautiful wife!"

"Good," I tell him, getting to my feet. "Because it's time to wake everyone. We have a lot of work to do."

CHAPTER TWENTY-FIVE

L ike any amazing place, the village of Leaf Scape was not built in a day. Or a month. Or a year, if ticking off the days from a human calendar.

But, in time, Leaf Scape provided all we needed to live fairly comfortable lives while maintaining the rehabilitative *worl* up the mountain. Couples were matched upon waking and enchanted so that it seemed as if they'd always been together. The community worked together fairly well, for the most part, building townhouse dwellings, setting the stones in the cobblestone aisles, erecting barns and fences, and creating the buildings necessary for ice, food, and body storage. The brilliant builders and architects I'd chosen were able to provide the village gardens with irrigation, as well as the homes with running water and flushing toilets.

Our community formed. I trained everyone how to identify and grow food and herbs. I taught Gavin how to create and activate medicines, infusing them with his magic to release their maximum potency. I showed him how to cure common maladies, and how to treat those injured or inflicted by the *scorched.*

All the other dwellers, I assigned as Witches and Warlocks and were trained how to handle the *scorched,* how to cast their healing energies into the *worl,* and how to replenish their internal source of energy by caring daily for their *notas.* Most excelled and became *Oracs,* highly skilled at handling the *scorched* and maintaining the protective barrier around the *worl.* Only a few were not well suited, and were classified as *unaccomplished,* though still found positions of use in the village.

Everyone worked. In the beginning, everyone was eager to pull together and help one another out, finding the positions where they could do the most good for the village as a whole, but as we all settled into our stations, the human condition leaked in. I had to settle more and more squabbles over jealousy, complaints of laziness or greed, arguments over rights to this house or that. I assigned Leonard Drake as the Head Warlock, and his serene wife, Decima, as Head Witch, and left them to govern the squabbles of their coven full of witches and warlocks.

The one thing no one complained about were their

spouses. Happily matched, once the village was established, everyone set about creating their families.

Including Gavin and me. We settled into our lives as the village Witch Doctor and his wife, and, as of two and a half weeks ago, we became parents to our baby girl, Indigo.

The cache of spells I had acquired for my mission are all but gone, so, luckily, there is less need for magic and only a bit of medical training left to do, but what is more concerning to me now is my dwindling supply of *gorne*. I rationed my supply so Indigo and I would be healthy through my entire pregnancy, but now, my store of *gorne* is so thin, I've had to talk more and more about our impending future.

I have warned Gavin I must return to the Abyss, and that he will have to stay in Leaf Scape and perform his work as Witch Doctor until Indigo comes of age and can be trained. Once she is ready to inherit the position, my husband can retire and join me in the Abyss.

But it will be a long time from now.

"I don't think you should be lifting so much." Gavin notes my huffing and puffing and takes the box of blown glass bottles from me.

"You don't need to worry. The breathlessness always goes away," I reassure him, although we both know, at some point it won't.

His lips fall into a hard line and he looks away. Fortune can no longer hide the truth.

"I just thought it might get better after Indigo was born," he says. "Since your lungs had room to expand again."

There's no point in discussing it again; he knows the shortness of breath has had nothing to do with my pregnancy. He knew it wouldn't go away with the birth, but he's continued to hope, on any possibility that presents itself, that our fate could change.

I cast a long gaze at our baby girl, asleep in the cradle the *Grandmother* trees created by reaching down their limbs and carefully interweaving their branches. Indigo sleeps most peacefully in the *Grandmother's* arms.

I could stare at our baby for hours. I treasure every chance I have to hold Indigo, to kiss her little cheeks and toes, or just watch her sleep, because three weeks is not enough time with her.

But then, no amount of time will ever be enough.

"You're still recovering," Gavin says, hefting the box onto the counter. "The breathing could still improve."

We've been working on rock extractions, emulsions, and herbal concoctions all morning—me blending them, him activating their potency. I return to the butcher's block slowly. I have to do everything more slowly, stopping to catch my breath often, and I try to ignore the new wheeze that has surfaced. I have strictly rationed out what is left of the *gorne,* trying to use less than what I need to be comfortable, because I want every second I can steal with my husband and daughter, even though the tips of my fingers and toes have started to turn a ghastly blue. The truth is, the *gorne* will run out soon and I cannot survive without it.

I do my best to draw a breath as I focus on Indigo's peaceful little face.

The pounding of hammers doesn't even stir our sweet child, as the builders erect more townhouses across the aisle from our abode. She is an incredibly easy baby, which I hope will make things easy on Gavin when I'm gone.

I take a bottle from the box and stuff the herbs I've chopped into the mouth of the bottle.

"I think all of the work we're doing now is going to be useful for you when I go," I say. "You won't have to worry about falling behind on anything for a while."

As usual, Gavin doesn't want to hear it. He ignores me, concentrating far harder than he needs to on activating the bottles of medicines in front of him. I know it's hard for him to maintain such a high level of denial, but I also know it's the only thing from keeping his heart from breaking.

I want to take it away. Stay forever. Breathe. Just breathe.

My heart broke the moment I swallowed the enchantment, since I knew what was to come, and it continues to crumble with every evidence of his sorrow.

"Gavin..."

"I don't want to talk about it, okay?"

"It's going to happen and this denial isn't helping—"

"Because I don't understand why you can't just get a lifetime supply of that *gorne* stuff and stay with me forever. You should be doing everything you can to stay here. Get a shipment of it sent here! You brought us all here...you brought *me* here to be with you! If you don't want to stay for me, than you should at least stay for Indigo!"

"It's not that easy to acquire and Gypsies can't go into dimensional atmospheres without it. That's how Lutte Jupiter became *scorched.* That's what started all our problems."

"That's what brought us together!" he says.

"And it is what keeps us apart. If we can eradicate *scorching* by rehabilitating those who are *scorched,* then there will be no need for Leaf Scape and you can be with me in the Abyss even sooner."

Talk of the Abyss frightens him, although he won't admit it. It's another human concept that doesn't allow him to believe he could ever live comfortably with me in a wagon in that dark place I call *home*, between the outer spaces.

I try again. "We need to talk about—"

"What we need to talk about is Drake and how much you let him get away with," he says, stopping his work to lean one hand on the counter. I'm willing to take his anger; I know it grows out of his pain. "It started when you let him change his name from Leonard to Leofflaud—"

"He felt it would help him embrace his role and it was harmless."

"Do you know he conjured a whole new wing to that mansion? And he's invited the Kettles' twins to clean for him? They wouldn't have to do that if the place wasn't so huge! I don't think it's fair. Not when everyone else is living in townhouses and he's living in a mansion!"

"The Kettles' twins are unaccomplished witches and, frankly, they weren't very good at any of the other jobs they've been assigned to. They seem happy to clean for the Drakes and I think it's fitting that the Head Warlock and Head Witch have a more substantial dwelling. Don't forget, they're storing a lot of the village odds and ends too."

"It's gluttonous," Gavin grumbles.

"Would you trade our dwelling for one like that? One that isn't surrounded by the joyful and healing vibrations of the *Grandmothers?*" The branches overhead wave their leaves in pleasure, as if a soft breeze is rolling through them.

The walls of our home, shop, and clinic, were created by the trunks of several Grandmothers, which all appeared a night after we arrived. At the end of the long aisle leading to the mountain, we found the *Grandmothers* standing tall, trunk to trunk, creating a fortress wall with all their bodies.

The *Grandmothers'* branches laced around one another, like hugs that continue to grow and grasp, and they laced together their branches over our heads to keep out the elements. We learned we could tie lesser-used items to their branches and the *Grandmothers* would tote them up high, concealing the items within their branches like a hidden attic. And with one sweet request, the *Grandmothers* are always willing to lift down the items too. On clear nights in the summer, they sometimes untangle their arms and reach skyward, giving up a gorgeous view of the moon, and when Gavin and I are busy, they always offer us a cradle of their branches and swing baby Indigo lovingly while we work.

Gavin and I fell in love with the house the first time we saw it. Leofflaud Drake did too, but it was quite obvious when we entered through one of the two curved arch doorways, that the charmed abode was meant for the village witch doctor and his family. One doorway led into the shop, the other into the clinic, and there were window holes all around and in the back where our living quarters would be. In direct line with the path off the mountain, and providing the natural light needed to grow some specialty herbs, the dwelling was as charming as it was charmed, but the living quarters were tiny. Two bedrooms, a bathroom, a living area combined with a counter space that seemed meant as a kitchen.

But Gavin still hasn't responded to my question. I know Leofflaud likes to brags about the mansion, and mostly Gavin isn't bothered by it, but every now and again, Leofflaud gets under his skin anyway.

"Should I remind you how much the Head Warlock wanted this house? And how the *Grandmothers* shoved him out when he declared he was keeping it for himself?"

Gavin chuffs a laugh at that. The *Grandmothers* didn't really shove Leofflaud, but rather, gently cupped their branches and pushed him out the door, leaving us inside. They'd made up their minds. They decided the house was ours.

"I don't know how Decima stands him," Gavin says, gathering bottles in his arms to store on the shelves lined between the shop and our back rooms. "She's such a good person, and an incredible witch. I don't know how she puts up with his bragging and grandstanding, much less agreed to have a child with him."

I know how she does it. The same way all the couples in the village do, including us. It's the only way these strangers would be loyal to one another, begin families, and populate our vital community.

My gypsy *enchantment potion* is as powerful as any spell. The potion mellows over time in such a way that Gavin no longer believes that little sip from my flask so long ago has anything to do with his feelings for me. The truth is that the enchantment only intensifies over time, lacing true feelings to the contrived ones, until the bond is nearly unbreakable.

That's why it's going to hurt so much and that's why we need to talk about how we're going to keep in touch, so we don't go insane being apart.

"I gave Grim Trimp and Larch Taus the pieces they use to travel out of Leaf Scape for supplies and I told them to guard them with their lives, because I can't just overnight more from the Abyss." After we came to Leaf Scape, I risked going into the *vias* to retrieve what I could of my broken, crystal ball. It was the only way the villagers could travel into their old Outer World for supplies without being lost in the *vias* forever. "But they still could lose them or break them, so I buried the box with the biggest piece out in the field. I've spelled the cabinet it's in too, so you and Indigo are the only ones who will be able to retrieve it in an emergency."

"Okay, fine," he says with a wary sigh. These aren't the conversations I want either of us to remember. Or the resentment we both feel, as if leaving is a choice. As if it doesn't shatter my heart.

Indigo wakes with a tiny whimper, as if she's displeased by our conversation too. The *Grandmother* cradle of branches extends my child to me and I pluck her from her cozy spot with a warm, "Thank you, *Grandmother.*"

The conversation is abandoned as I hold my daughter to my heart, focusing on keeping the oxygen in my lungs as I listen with eyes closed to her precious cooing.

CHAPTER TWENTY-SIX

I t happens exactly the way I knew it would.

It is the middle of the night. I am startled awake.

I can't breathe.

My mouth gapes, my lungs won't expand.

Gavin snores softly beside me, exhausted from the hard day of work.

Even if he were awake, he can't help me.

I struggle to gulp some air, desperate to will some oxygen into my body, but nothing comes.

I roll off the bed and land on the floor. No sound comes out of me; there is no breath to exhale.

I saved the last spell for this moment. It was cast for me at a high, but worthwhile price, into an empty eggshell, which I've left beneath the bed, exactly in my reach, as I knew it would need to be. When I crack the shell on my sternum, the spell will rush out and engulf me. I will be instantly transported back to the Abyss, to the home that no longer feels like it is mine.

My home is here, beside the man who hasn't awaken yet, and the baby who suddenly whimpers from the Grandmother cradle beside our bed.

My eyes bulge like hard boiled eggs. I feel the veins in my neck strain upward, searching for air, making ridges in my skin.

I can't propel myself to my feet. I can't lift Indigo from her cradle for one last embrace.

The corners of my eyes squeeze out trails of tears that soak into my hair.

I am fading. The room is graying at the edges.

I need to break the egg shell on my chest. I need to do it now, before it is too late to do anything.

Indigo whimpers again. Her tiny fist quivers over the edge of the cradle as if she would help me if she could.

I can't bring myself to leave her.

All I want is another moment to share the same space, remembering the smell of my daughter, the velvet of her skin, the kiss of my husband, the width of his hand as it envelopes mine.

Leaving them seems like a worse death then fading away in their presence, but if I die here right now, it is a guarantee that I will never see them again.

I have to give us a chance. Even if it is centuries from now, at least, I will see them again.

Panic struggles into my veins and my nervous system revolts, battling an invisible enemy. I flounder on the floor. I try to reach for the egg, but my arms don't respond to my commands.

Death is coming for me. The gray edges close in like a drawstring bag.

A blurry wisp of a *Grandmother*'s branch reaches over my head. The limb scoops up the egg between two, tender, finger-like curls of bark.

Tears flow down my temples and clog my ears.

The delicate fingers of the *Grandmother* branch places the egg on my sternum.

A tendril of bark caresses my cheek, and with one gentle downward push, the branch shatters the egg, and I am transported back to the Abyss.

THE END

Want to continue reading?
Preorder CAST Here!
Releases February 22nd, 2019.

If you have a moment, please review *Forecast* at the store

where you purchased it. Help other fantasy readers by telling them what you enjoyed about the book. Thank you!

You are also formally invited to join my reader group on Facebook: Misty's Book Babes. Come and get the latest on releases, sneak previews of covers, extras, and great conversation!

PREVIEW OF CAST

THE SECOND STORY IN THE CAST SERIES

CHAPTER ONE

I could say that what happened was accidental, that I had no choice, but the truth is, there's always a choice.

A little bit of that truth is that I misplaced my foot on the edge of a cobblestone, my ankle turned, and my heel slipped off the side. A delightful part of that truth is that I swayed toward Rune Drake, and his hand shot out to grasp my arm so I wouldn't fall. The terrible part is that we locked eyes the moment it happened and he snatched his fingers back, but the air had already vanished from my lungs.

The last time I touched Rune Drake, we were twelve years old and there were no consequences.

Things are so very different now.

We're nearly eighteen, and the cost of a forbidden touch in our village is exile.

The night started off so normally, I never imagined this could happen.

As with every celebration, the village square was packed. The entire coven of Magical came out to honor the small group of graduating Magicians on their advancement to Wizards and Wizardesses and to enjoy the extensive buffet provided by the graduates' families. The smoky scent of stew blended with the freshness of the coming fall, quickening my step as I entered the square.

Parties have always been my favorite. I love the hum of greetings and friendly conversations all around me. It makes me feel more a part of our village than I may ever be. Every face I glimpsed, as I made my way through the coven crowd was as familiar as my own. It's easy to snuggle into the hospitable ambience of Leaf Scape when there's a party.

The crowd wandered loosely from one banquet table to the next with me bobbing in the midst of them. The graduates' families heckled one another over the somewhat-friendly competition to present the most tantalizing contribution to the overall meal.

The Brinches put out wisteria wine and cucumber seltzers, coconut tea and iced caramel coffee in hand-painted cups; the Shafes had platters of steaming pasties and savory stew; the Druges supplied bowls of kale, spinach, and wilting arugula, with glass decanters full of raspberry vinegar, lilac salt, and lemon-infused oil. But, as usual, it was the Bluglas' table was bound to win the complimentary nod from the Head Warlock. They had an ocean-themed table this year, with puffer fish made of horned melon and schools of Gak seeds swimming in various shades of honeydew and Crenshaw slices. The centerpiece was a frenzy of vicious, watermelon sharks diving up from the table with open mouths full of jagged, white teeth.

I heaped my plate twice, but no matter how delicious it all was, there was only so much eating I could do.

Then the dancing began and I was left with absolutely nothing to do.

Coven rule is that Magical boys are required to keep to the East side of the square, while all of us girls stay to the West edge. Elders, mothers, and fathers can drift back and forth between the separated groups as they please, but *given* couples and bound couples are the only ones allowed to come together and dance in the middle of the square.

At the first whistle of Lady Kettle's flute, tables were cleared away to make room for the dancers. My entire peer group—they're called *shibbers*—jumped up and skittered into the growing middle area, pairing up with their *givens*. Dancing in clumps is acceptable for couples, as long as *givens* only touch one another.

But since my *given* doesn't live in the village, I could either dance by myself or not at all.

The tables at the west side of the square were empty, except for the ones occupied by Elders, *youngers,* or the young Magicians. If I asked, most of the Elders would have pulled up a chair for me—but that's only if I wanted my *shibbers* to laugh at me for sitting with their parents. Or, I could've entertained the *youngers* with piggy-back rides across the dance floor, which I've done once or twice before on desperate occasions, when I couldn't bear to be left on the outskirts of the celebration.

Tonight, I opted to weave my way through the empty tables to the west wall and pull myself up to sit alone, swinging my feet and watching the revelry from a distance.

Usually, I amuse myself by watching all my *shibbers,* while keeping an eye out for Rune, but the lightening stones around the square were uncharacteristically dim since we've been without a good storm for the past couple weeks. The glow made sifting through the dancers a lot harder.

My gaze drifted from the banquet tables to the dance floor and back again. I considered a cup of coconut tea, but was too full and too lazy to pick my way across the square to get it.

I yawned, and Rune Drake caught my eye, standing at the Bluglas' table by himself. He slipped a hunk of watermelon shark into his mouth from between his fingers. I looked away before anyone else could catch me staring, but my eyes darted back just as fast. Rune flashed me a tiny grin and flicked his chin away from the crowded square.

I knew exactly what it meant.

I slipped over the far side of the West Wall and escaped around the brick corner of townhouse #83. Rune followed moments later. We slipped down Long Aisle, the most lengthy and most romantic street in the whole village. Once out of view, we joined up to walk side-by-side, glancing over our shoulders every other second to be sure we weren't being followed.

Being out of view is a significant feat, but staying that way in a village as small as Leaf Scape is another. The din of the revelry faded behind the brick barricade of the connected, townhouse walls.

"We made it," Rune whisper-laughed.

The thrill of being alone with him shot through my stomach. It was the same thrill I've felt since the age of seven, when we discovered each other sneaking out to explore the village after the night bell had rung, signaling that everyone should be locked in for the night.

After that first night, we met up a lot more to explore every crack and crevice of the village and discover its peculiarities, including stuff like Lady Edith Earl's proclivity for lying around naked in the moonlight on the

Grandfather rocks; a charmed patch of sugar cane that can only be accessed by conjuring a recipe that calls for it; the small wooden cabinet—with a thin trapezoid carved in its door—sunk deep into the soil at the back of the Eastern garden, which contains a sizeable chunk of clear glass that couldn't be broken or removed; the breathtaking, Moon Swing that can do a complete, white-knuckling, 360-degree turn over its own trapeze bar; the spelled slingshots, dredged from Lake Tinneret, that makes stones into shooting stars with such fierce accuracy that we thought of throwing them back into the water.

When we reached twelve years of age, our *shibbers* were separated by sex and required to remain that way. Only boys and girls who were *given* to one another could mingle. Rune and I were experienced enough with navigating the village at night that we didn't worry about being caught together, but there were other changes that persuaded us to be more careful about following a different rule.

Rune became swiftly aware that my chest had become fascinatingly lumpy. Unfamiliar shivers made my knees unstable whenever I stared too long at his thickening arms, or the emerging shadow on his chin and around his lips. All I ever wanted to do was look at him, and while it wasn't exactly against any rule to *look*, staring at a non-*given* of the opposite sex was completely unacceptable. I had absolutely no reason to look at any of my male *shib-*

bers, so I mastered the art of stealing glances of Rune in public, drinking in his details privately, when we snuck out together at night.

Neither of us ever mentioned it, but the changes messed with our dynamic. We were suddenly out of sync. Who went up a tree first became an awkward issue of both fashion and equality; uncontrollable blushing became a thing; a weird modesty overshadowed our swims in Lake Tinneret together; and then there was this foreign ache that anchored itself deep in my stomach whenever I hadn't seen Rune for a couple days.

It was obvious that we were no longer who we had been. Our bodies were different, how we treated each other was different, the unrelenting thoughts of kissing him was...*very* different. Daydreams about Rune were as abundant as rain and always splashing into my head.

I believe that's what made obeying the terrifying new mandate—non-*given*s were forbidden to touch after the age of twelve—a fairly easy choice. Especially when the infraction could be punishable by exile.

It's not that I didn't think about breaking the law. I thought about it at least a dozen times a day, with my hands or fingers or lips. Rune winced when he told me he thought about it too, his face hidden in the moonlit branches of a cemetery *grandmother* tree, but we never attempted it.

Despite keeping our hands to ourselves in the last six

years, the law never suppressed the thrill that crashes over me every time I see Rune. The rush itself may be momentary, but the residual tingle never leaves. It is a wild, untamable thing that has lived in my skin since we were children.

The usual tingle prickled down my arms as we strolled down Long Aisle at dusk. It should have been warning enough. The wise thing, to keep us both safe, would have been to turn back to the party in the square.

We didn't.

Long aisle was washed in the golden, flickering glow of lightening stones, nestled in second floor townhouse windows. The stones' dim light swept down the lush ivy tucked with colorful blooms and spilled over the striped awnings like honey. Rune buried his fists in his pockets. His lightening bug *nota,* Twinkle, flashed near his temple, casting a green glow on his skin. Harmony, the humming bird he inherited from his mother, appeared over one shoulder before zipping away.

I glimpsed the ridges of muscle in his tense arms as we continued to walk. I locked my hands behind me. A meandering breeze circulated perfume from Lady Brinch's cascading wisteria and mixed it with the delightful, ever-lingering scent of fresh bread and sweets from Lady Bint's bakery.

I tried to think of the law.

I swear I did.

But I didn't try very hard.

Mostly, I considered how exciting it was to walk down Long Aisle with Rune, and how ducking into its shadows with him would be mind blowing.

I walked too close to him, I knew it, but I loved the sound of our footsteps on the cobblestones. Our synchronicity was hypnotic. I bobbed awkwardly toward him, but caught myself each time, before we could collide. His hand shot up too, even though he jerked it away before making contact.

I thought about falling into his arms. Lovely spikes of adrenaline stirred the flutters in my stomach at the thought.

Rune smiled with every near miss, as if maybe he felt it too.

I know I should've angled away, but I was magnetized. It's hard enough to fight against something you want, but downright impossible to resist what you need, and I have needed Rune Drake's easy smile, his kindness, his maturity, his brilliance, as long as I have known him.

The moment overwhelmed me. I stepped on a crooked cobblestone and tumbled sideways. I caught myself, but Rune's fingertips curled around my arm, warm, steady, and strong. He let go as quickly as he made contact, but it was too late.

I gasped.

So did Rune.

And that's why we're standing in the shadows of an

unlit Long Aisle awning, staring at each other like we just sealed our fate. Or, our death sentence.

Touching him seemed like a hugely romantic notion, but now that it's happened, I can't breathe.

Rune shoots a glance up, and then down, Long Aisle, searching for witnesses. My stomach drops as I scan the aisle too. I don't see anyone, but that doesn't mean we haven't been seen. On a regular day, villagers will pop out of the ivy-draped arcades; they appear on the flower-camouflaged stoops like magic tricks; they burst from windows like jack-in-the-box toys. I know from experience, they could be anywhere and, so often, they are.

We stand in the street, waiting to be caught. Waiting for someone to shout our names. Waiting for someone to yell at us to get away from each other.

It's so silent, I'm pretty sure Rune is holding his breath right along with me.

No one shouts. Nobody yells.

An overhead lightening stone fizzles out in a blink, startling us both. Rune exhales at the same time I do.

"That was my fault," I say. My voice drops and my lips tremble with the guilt. I *meant* to walk too close. I wanted his touch in any greedy way I could get it. I knew I was breaking the law and I did it anyway.

Rune ducks down, catching my gaze in his before straightening up. He drags my eyes along with him. He's smiling.

"Don't be sorry," he whispers, his attention rivets on me as if he can look nowhere else. "Ever," he adds.

Stupidly, impulsively, I reach for his hand. We just escaped complete disaster, and here I am, without a downward glance, running straight at it again. Moths have a better chance of avoiding a bonfire than I have of leaving Rune Drake alone. My heart thunks at the base of my throat, partly because I'm breaking the law, but mostly because I'm terrified he'll come to his senses and pull away.

He doesn't.

Rune fingers thread through mine and with the tiniest tug, he pulls our bodies closer than we've been in six years. Our fingers laced, sandwiched between us, the top of our hands rest against each other's thighs. Mine brushes the hard cord of muscle in his leg. Rune bows his head toward mine.

This is it.

My first kiss.

I like to think it will be his too.

He closes his eyes and I shut mine, rising up on my toes to close the gap between us. I inhale the clean scent of him mixed with the ambrosia of ivy blossoms and cinnamon roll pastries. I never imagined it could be this perfect.

"*Mirers!*" a familiar voice barks from the mouth of the aisle, shattering the moment.

ACKNOWLEDGMENTS

THANK YOU, GOD, for my every blessing of family, friends, and this beautiful life. It is always about you.

THANK YOU SO MUCH TO my cover designer and twin-from-another-womb, M.R. Polish. Your talents blow me away and it's like you're my twin or something…lol

HUGE THANKS TO Casey Bond for all the positive vibes, the yoga recommendations, and the positivity that helped me finish this story. You inspire me in a thousand different ways and I am grateful to call you my friend.

SHOUT OUT TO my incredible beta team: Jes Ekker, and Casey Bond. Thank you for the straight-talk feed back that has made Forecast stronger, and your willingness to read on hardly any notice at all. Love you, ladies!

U.P. YAHs and love to Marcia & Larry Joosten for all the hospitality and info about their hometown. Hope I did Lake Linden proud.

Special thanks to Cheer Stephenson-Papworth and her Band of Dystopian for helping to get the Caste Series into the world. I see how tirelessly you work to connect authors and fans and deeply admire your passion.

Thank you to Tia & Brittany for their edits and suggestions on the short-story version of Forecast, which I eventually re-wrote into this fuller novella. Talented and timely, these ladies are the real deal!

Hugs and love to my Facebook reader group, Misty's Book Babes. Thank you, Babes, for reading, sharing, reviewing, and always making me giggle. I am grateful for every one of you!

END OF THE BOOK BALONEY

So, readers often like to know about the story behind the stories I write. Stuff like: why did I write this book? Where did the idea come from? What process did I use? What was my life like while writing this story? What's the blooper reel of drafts look like?

If you go hard-core nerd (like I do) on this stuff, then get your glasses on! I'm about to give you some behind-the-keyboard details that nobody else will ever care about.

This book was three years in the making. I started and stopped with it too many times to count, because I hadn't realized my priorities were trying to shift me over to a happier place.

I'd been going whole-hog at writing and publishing and loving it, but I also poured my whole self into it. I was starting to feel a little hollow and I started to realize my

END OF THE BOOK BALONEY

folks are getting older. My kids are growing up. My husband has had to run out for pizza too many times. That kind of thing. I'd gotten out of whack.

So, I made getting balanced again my priority.

After I released Weeds of Detroit as Misty Paquette, I took a two-year break. Kind of. I mean, I never stop writing, because that's just something I do. Eat, sleep, brush my teeth, write. But in the time when I stopped publishing, I slowly formed a routine to bring myself back into a place of balance and joy. I started exercising regularly, meditating more frequently, hanging out with the family even more, and cooking more meals at home so we're all healthier and wealthier.

But the Caste Series was scritching at the back of my head the whole time too. I had planted a seed of this series in my previous series, The Dimension Thieves, when I introduced Lutte Jupiter and his background story. I always knew I was going to write more about Lutte, but I didn't know when.

Guess there's no time like the present, huh?

I got serious with the book in 2018 and spent months creating outlines for the entire series. There are nine books, not including the prequel. If we get that far. If the stories are well received, we'll keep on truckin'. But who knows...I might keep on going even if they aren't.

Forecast began as a short story of ten thousand words that I wrote for an anthology I did with a few author friends of mine. The book was called, *The Peculiar Lives of Circus Freaks* and we released it to mesh with the circus freak theme of the 2017 Utopia Conference we all attended in Nashville, TN.

By the time we discontinued the anthology, I had written *Cast* and figured I'd release the short again as a prequel or use it in *Cast* as a ridiculously long prologue.

Ultimately, I did neither, but rewrote the short into the story you've just read. I wanted to offer a prequel for free, and I wanted it to be a full story that would whet the reader's appetite for the rest of the Caste Series I have in store. I hope you've enjoyed it and now you have it: where I was, what I was doing, and how we got right here. Thanks for reading!

Young Adult Paranormal Fantasy
THE CORNERSTONE SERIES
#1 Cornerstone
#2 Keystone
#3 Jamb
#4 Capstone

Young Adult Sci-Fantasy
THE DIMENSION THIEVES SERIES
Book One (Episodes 1-3)
Book Two (Episodes 4-6)
Book Three (Episodes (7-9)
Book Four (Episodes 10-12)

Young Adult Urban Fantasy
MERCY

Young Adult Novella
A SHIFT IN LOYALTY

ADULT BOOKS BY MISTY PAQUETTE

Literary Fiction

WEEDS of DETROIT

STRONGER

Science-Fantasy

THE FLY HOUSE

Contemporary Romance

THE CROSSED & BARED SERIES

HALE MAREE (Book One)

FULL OF GRACE (Book Two)

Erotica

THE BROWN BAG SERIES

THE RELEASE CLUB

*Misty Provencher writing as Misty Paquette

ABOUT THE AUTHOR

Misty Provencher is a prolific writer who creates fantasy stories for young adult readers and up. She also writes contemporary romance for adults under the name Misty Paquette.

While Provencher can ride a motorcycle, knows how to karate chop, and has learned enough French, Spanish, and sign language to get herself slapped, Misty's life is dedicated to connecting with, and understanding, the people who cross her path. She is totally enchanted with the world and spends her days trying to translate her everyday muses into words.

Misty Provencher lives in the mitten. Knock on her internet door at the following addresses, or find her wherever great coffee is sold:

For more information:
mistyprovencherauthor.com
misty@mistyprovencherauthor.com
You are also invited to join her Facebook Reader Group:
Misty's Book Babes

Made in the USA
Middletown, DE
31 January 2019